I0721897

For Rose and Ellen, the coolest women I know

SUNSET CHRONICLES

HANGING MOON

PAUL STEPHENSON

HOLLOW STONE

Copyright © 2021 by Paul Stephenson

All rights reserved.

No portion of this book may be reproduced in any form without written permission from the publisher or author, except as permitted by U.S. copyright law.

This version published 2024

Note for readers

The Sunset Chronicles is a monthly sci fi serial. Think of it like a series, much like you'd get on your favourite tv streaming service. There are seasons, split up into episodes (five per season). Each episode is designed to be read in roughly two hours, though fast readers may blast through them even quicker, and those who like to really get stuck into the story may take longer. They're intended to be thrilling and exciting, and are released regularly each month so that you can keep up with the story even if you have a hectic schedule. And who doesn't, these days? It's perfect for if you want to slip some space horror into your lunch break, or if you want to binge it of an evening.

If you've come to this book first, please check out episode one, *Last Light*, which is available in print and ebook.

Also, although *The Sunset Chronicles* is a story that stretches from the ice moon of Europa to every corner of the globe, its author remains English. As such, international readers should note that spellings are of the UK variation of English, so if you see a typo, it must be because of that.

If you're in the UK and you see a typo, it must be your imagination.

Chapter One

The smell of dinner wafting down the Minos into the flight module reminded Wyn she'd not eaten anything since waking from her enforced slumber. Her stomach cramped in agreement. Reclaimed carbon may taste like shit, but if you stuck enough chemical flavouring in, it didn't smell too bad. Once they were under the ice, she'd cook. Stef had taken on the duty for the whole mission so far, but she'd be too busy, and Wyn might be able to show them some of Baba's skills.

'Miles, run these calculations for me, will you?' she asked the empty room.

'Yes, Commander.'

She stretched, bones weary and aching from years without gravity. She should go see Barnes again, see about getting one of his magic injections. She sure as shit shouldn't try pulling off the most complex manoeuvres in the history of manned flight with aching joints.

The smell pulled the rest of the crew away from their respective tasks. They floated toward the mess to find the Captain himself cooking. Wyn identified the smell as grilled hamburgers, or as close to it as they'd get from insect protein.

'What's cooking, Cap?' Barnes asked, rubbing his stomach absent-mindedly as he entered from the men's rack.

'Jesus, Doc,' the Captain replied. 'You look like hammered shit.'

'Nice to see you, too, Captain,' Barnes replied with a crooked smile, before easing himself into a seat at the table.

Wyn pulled up next to him. 'Hey,' she whispered. 'You think you could hook me up with one of your magic jabs?'

'Commander,' he replied loud enough to make her wince. 'I am a serious, trained medical professional. I do not simply hook up one with medication. I am not your dealer.' He cracked out a wide smile. 'What is it? Bone ache?'

She nodded.

'Come see me after the feast.'

'Burgers,' the Captain called. 'Come get 'em.' He served up the food into tin trays. There were burgers, corn cobs, grits, all made out of the same crushed bugs. They looked real enough, however, and after four years, this amounted to a feast. 'We're blowing out the ration limit for the evening.'

'Great,' Stef said. 'I'm going to be too full to fit in my space suit.'

'Mmm, full of bugs,' Barnes said, sneering at the tray.

'Hey,' Zoe said, taking the tray with a great deal more enthusiasm. 'Don't knock bug food. Your body doesn't care where you're getting your protein from.'

'My taste buds do,' Barnes said, sticking his fork into his grits.

'Barnes, are you going to throw your food across the room again?' Li asked, mouth half full of burger. 'Because I've got too much shit to do to be cleaning bits of your dinner out of the air reclaimators.'

'Li, my good man. I wouldn't dream of it.'

'Hamza,' Stef said, twirling a corn cob round on her fork, marvelling at its design. 'I've been wondering. Is this halal? I thought insects were...'

'Not Haram?' Hamza replied. 'There's a lot of debate. Some scholars forbid eating insects, because they're assumed to be dirty. But the world went and changed on us. You'll find plenty of Muslims who say reclaimed carbon is an affront to Allah, but it's remarkable how many of them live in countries the Mar hasn't reached yet. As for the rest of us, well, my cleric had one thing to say about it. 'Allah wants you to live.' So, I live.'

Stef considered this for a moment with mouth full of corn, before frowning. 'Doesn't answer my question,' she said.

'You noticed, huh?' He smiled, and turned to Wyn. 'So, Commander, we going to crash into Jupiter, or what?'

'Yeah,' Barnes said, 'fucker sure is big.'

'Not if I can help it,' Wyn replied, her mouth full of hamburger.

'Good news,' Captain Davis added, having finally dished out his own meal and joined his crew.

Ermine finished his food without a word and stood, taking his plate over to the dishwasher. Zoe's gaze followed the XO's arse. Wyn had never found the right moment to discuss the biologist's obvious infatuation with the XO, and wasn't sure she could keep her lunch down having it. One to tackle on the way home, perhaps. With the Minos pointed toward Earth with a cargo hold full of cure, who knew what kinds of office romances might spring up. Not that there were any candidates as far as Wyn was concerned. She enjoyed the drama of it all, though.

'What's up, Li?' Zoe asked, tearing her gaze away from Ermine's admittedly pert posterior.

'Li's always glum looking,' Stef said, nudging her fellow engineer.

'Must be my natural face,' Li replied. He offered a half smile. 'I'm tired.'

'Aren't we all?' Hamza chipped in.

'Oh, I don't know,' Wyn said. 'I feel pretty well rested.'

A few embarrassed chuckles went around the room, and Wyn joined them. She must be over it. There were bigger things to worry about.

At the head of the table, the Captain watched everyone eat their food and rib each other gently, chuckling each time the doctor ostentatiously pulled faces at the terrible food. He looked more relaxed and satisfied than he had all trip, a mood which spread around the crew. Whatever disharmony remained in the wake of Sunset's course corrections, they'd turned it into positive energy.

Once Ermine cleared the plates, the Captain leaned forward, and the crew's conversations fell away.

'It's a strange feeling,' he said, in his low Midwestern drawl. 'I feel it too. Four years and counting. Two years of planning before. We've had curveballs thrown at us, but we've dealt with them as I knew we would. It comes down to this. Everything we've ever done in our lives. Hours in classrooms. Flight school. College. Every stupid decision, every doomed relationship, every right turn, every wrong one. It all led us here.

'Tomorrow, we're going to become the first people in the history of our species to walk on the surface of a moon that's not our own. We're going to operate the first ever interplanetary mining operation. And, in all likelihood, we're going to be the first contact for microbial life. With luck, patience, and hard work, we'll head home the saviours of our planet. Make no mistake about it, people. The history books will remember us.'

'Unless Wyn crashes us into Jupiter,' Barnes said, making Hamza snort across the table.

Wyn threw a piece of fake corn at him.

'You're here for a reason,' the Captain continued. 'You deserve to be here. Trust in yourselves. Trust in your crew. Let's get this done, and get what we came for. Okay?'

Nods of sage agreement went around the crew. Even Ermine gave a barely perceptible nod of approval. The Captain stood, and Hamza clapped him on the back.

'Well,' he said. 'I guess that's why they made you Captain.'

'That and he's old,' Stef said.

'Okay, okay,' Captain Davis said. 'Get back to it. But I want everyone in bunk by twenty-three-hundred tonight, okay? Goes for you, too, Commander.'

Wyn rolled her eyes.

'If anyone here catches Wyn with a coffee in her hand before tomorrow morning, you have my permission to stick her out of the airlock. We'll get Miles to fly us to the surface.'

'I wouldn't advise it, Captain,' Miles's voice crackled out of the speaker.

'Don't worry, Miles,' Wyn said. 'He's too fond of me. Plus, there'd be paperwork to fill out.'

'I am relieved,' Miles responded.

'Wyn,' Li Wei said. 'You want to go over the landing sequence with us one last time?'

'Sure.'

They left the comfort of the mess hall, Wyn following Li and Stef through the heavy door to the ship's rear. Stepping into the cavernous expanse of the Minos's cargo hold fucked with Wyn's equilibrium. Coming from the cramped main section of the ship—where it was awkward for two people to pass each other—into a room the size of an aircraft hangar was disconcerting.

Despite its size, there wasn't much empty space. Neatly lining the sides were food reserves, whirring air reclaimators, and the huge tanks feeding fuel into the main thrusters. Stacked atop them were cases holding everything they might need, from medicine to spare clothes.

Separate still, and covering every inch of floor space, was everything they'd need on the surface. Stood in the middle, resplendent in its crap design, was their ticket down to the surface.

The shuttle was officially called the Androgeus, named for the son of Minos in Greek mythology. But nobody called it that. On the second day of training, Hamza had called it the Andy, and it had stuck.

Most of the people working in the ISS had the same preoccupation as NASA with naming things after Greek mythology. So, everything to do with the mission was somehow tied in with Europa. Except it didn't work so well in practical terms. Minos was the King of Crete, son of Zeus and Europa. He had a taste for boiling people alive and sending people into the labyrinth to face the Minotaur. Oh, and when he died, he became a gatekeeper for hell. Not a nice chap, but they still named a boat after him. As for Androgeus, he got brutally murdered, which was always a good omen.

'Hello, handsome,' Wyn said, approaching the shuttle. The Andy was an ugly little brute, but tough. Designed with functionality in mind, he was the sole piece of hardware specifically designed for this mission, rather than repurposed out of space junk from abandoned Mars missions. It would take the whole crew down from the Minos to the surface of the moon, where it would have to survive temperatures below fifty kelvins, and the intense radiation of Jupiter's magnetotail. It had to be able to take back off and carry them back to the Minos. And there was the small matter of it having to hold an entire underwater habitat, called the Haven, and the drilling equipment needed to get it under the ice. They'd leave the habitat and the drills behind, but hopefully carry tonnes of samples back.

She turned to the others. 'So, is our boy ready to go?'

'All set,' Li replied, checking a readout on his pad to make sure. 'Let's go through the sequence once more.'

Wyn nodded. 'Tomorrow morning I start the slingshot around Jupiter, use her gravity to build up speed, shoot us directly into Europa's orbit. We'll come in about two thousand clicks ahead, and we'll close the gap with thrusters. All told, it's a six-hour manoeuvre.'

Stef took over. 'Once in orbit, we'll move the crew through here, get the remaining equipment loaded, prep for descent. Li will prep the cargo bay launch sequence.'

'I've timed the whole sequence to seventeen minutes and thirteen seconds,' Li said. 'Fastest I've got it. We can start as soon as you join us.'

Wyn sighed. It felt too flabby. They had so little time before the magnetotail crested the horizon and cooked them.

'What if we move the crew through before I start the manoeuvre? It's six hours strapped into the Andy, but they're going to want to suit up anyway, in case anything goes wrong. Why not do it here? As soon as I'm in orbit, you start the sequence without me. I can get down here in time.'

Stef frowned. 'Could save a hell of a lot of time. Half an hour, if we're lucky. But you're going to have to haul ass down here. Once we start the launch sequence, we can't shut it down.'

'Captain Davis can do the pre-flight checks on the Andy, all that's left is the drop,' Wyn said.

'Easy,' Stef said.

'Piece of cake,' Li agreed.

The three of them looked up at the Andy.

'There's so much can go wrong,' Wyn said. 'We've not run this enough. What if I can't lock into an orbit, and have to stay up here?'

'The Captain flies us down. It's not like he's not got the experience,' Stef said.

'What if I can't find a good landing spot? What if I land where the ice is too thin? Or too close to a fissure, and unstable? Or too thick to drill? What if we can't get under before the magneto-tail...'

'What if elephants didn't have trunks?' Li interjected.

Stef laughed. 'Is that some kind of ancient Chinese proverb?'

Li smiled. 'No. Just trying to get her to shut up. It's going to be fine, Wyn. Or it's not. Worst comes to the worst we get back in the Andy and bug out.'

'If you say so,' Wyn said, looking at her feet. 'When do I suit up?'

'You can wait until you get down here, if you want,' Stef said. 'Flight control has separated pressure, so you're not at so much risk. Or, you could do the manoeuvre suited up, shave an extra few minutes off?'

Wyn frowned. 'I suppose it wouldn't interfere too much with the navigational controls. Might even help on some of the hard turns. It's just, those suits...'

'Clunky, I know.'

'It's fine.'

'Good. When we're under the ice, you get to chill out. Kick back and relax for a few days, let the rest of us do the hard work.'

'I can catch up on some sleep.'

Stef gave her a hug, and Li gave his own equivalent—a barely perceptible nod of the head.

Wyn said her goodnights and climbed back through to the reassuringly cramped space of the main deck. She looked across at the racks and thought about climbing in, but she needed to go over the numbers one last time, to be sure. If she didn't, she'd lie awake worrying about them. Besides, she'd left Miles to render the final vectors in her absence, and the crew probably wouldn't like it if she left the final checks to an experimental artificial intelligence who sounded permanently half cut.

Climbing back into the flight module, the view beyond the glass stopped the breath halfway out her throat. The swirling gas atmosphere of Jupiter broiled away, its vast colour palette filling every inch of the sky.

Easing into her seat, she checked the instrumentation. They were well within Jupiter's enormous gravitational field, pulling them inexorably toward its gassy surface.

Right on cue.

How the hell was she supposed to sleep, with views like this on offer? She could turn the engines off and within two days they'd sink into the enormous cloud, falling to a terrifying doom. A tiny part of her wanted to know what it felt like.

She picked up a pad, and checked the calculations.

'It's accurate to within three feet,' Miles said.

'I'm not questioning your abilities, Miles.'

'But you humans need the physical experience of seeing for yourself.'

'Exactly.'

'So, once you've checked the calculations, you'll be heading to the rack to get some sleep?'

'I don't feel like it,' she said, eyes drawn from the pad back to the view. 'But sure.'

There was a knock on the hatch. 'Wow,' Ermine said. 'Hell of a view.'

Wyn didn't turn round. 'None quite like it. Can I help you, XO?'

'Wanted to wish you luck tomorrow,' he said.

'Thanks.'

He fell silent, but Wyn could still sense him looming. The hairs on her neck still stood to attention, for one thing.

'Look,' he said, the conciliatory tone in his voice vanishing. 'I'm sorry about the other night.'

'Apology accepted,' Wyn replied. There was no forgiveness in her voice, as there had been no contrition in his. He'd confirmed it was his decision to drug her, not the Captain, which meant she felt a bit better. She hated Ermine already, so there was a little less hurt than before.

'I did what I thought was right for the mission. That's my job. The Captain gets to make the rousing speeches, while I'm the one who has to keep things running smoothly around here.'

'Understood.' She was not about to rise to the bait, no matter how tempting it might be.

He loomed silently for a moment longer. 'Fine,' he said. He turned to leave, but whatever bee was in his bonnet wouldn't let him. 'Do you know what?' he said, more snarl than anything else. 'I don't have to be liked by you. I don't have to be liked by anyone on this crew. I honestly could give a shit. I'm here for the mission, not to make pals. The mission. You endangered it, so I acted. End of story.'

She turned her chair. Her face was a few inches from his. 'You keep telling yourself that,' she hissed back at him. 'Nice apology, by the way. Clearly your subconscious has a problem with you drugging women without consent, or you wouldn't have come here offering what passes for an apology.'

'It wasn't my...'

'An apology I accepted, by the way,' she continued, barrelling over his attempt to argue against her. 'I know why you did it, because I'm not an idiot. I don't agree with you, or the Captain, but I understand it. But you couldn't bear the thought I might still think you were wrong, so you've trampled over your apology. And now you can stick it up your arse.'

He stood there a moment longer, simmering. Wyn turned back to her pad and did the same. She thought of another barb to throw at him, but when she turned back, he was gone.

She exhaled, loudly, and took a second to compose herself. What a prick.

'Miles, I'm going to bed. Wake me up if there's a deviance.'

'Yes, Commander.'

'I mean it,' she said. 'Any deviance.'

She made her way through to the rack. Zoe and Stef were both in their beds, curtains drawn. Stef's light shone through her curtain, and Wyn briefly considered trying to start a conversation, but thought better of it. She kicked her shoes off, climbed into her bunk, and pulled the curtain closed.

Turning on to her side, she stared at the wall, still seething. She forced her eyes closed, and tried to sleep.

Chapter Two

'Calm down,' Findlay said, his attention more on the pieces of tech in the bottom of Lois's bag than on the mad woman pacing around the hotel room fast enough to burn a trail into the cheap shag carpet.

'I'm telling you, Findlay, they knew. I don't know how I got out of there alive, let alone with my tech intact. But they fucking knew. They took me out so fast I'm amazed my feet touched the ground.'

'You think you might be overreacting?'

'I was there. When you hear that conversation, you'll see for yourself. It went from warm vibes to the Antarctic in about fifteen seconds.'

'I'm sorry,' he said. 'Bad choice of words. But you're basing this off a caught look. Burgess could have been telling him anything. There are plenty of reasons a man of his stature might need to get out of a meeting.'

She shook her head. 'I want my family out of the city. Tonight.'

'Lois, they let you out of the building. The only explanation is that you're wrong. Trust me, these people don't fuck about. They have their own fucking army, for God's sake. If they thought you were even remotely a threat, they would burst in that door.'

'Even more reason to get my family the hell out of here.'

'Let's see what their next move is.'

She sighed, continuing to pace. 'At least tell me you got the data dump you wanted.'

'Give me a chance,' he said. He connected attachments to the pad from her bag, and the data collector from her suit. He peered at his own pad for a moment, frowning.

Lois paced some more, which didn't help, but did at least constitute action of some kind. All she could think of was goons in black military gear breaking in her door and taking her girls away.

'Shit,' Findlay said, finally, still peering at his screen.

'What?'

'The data dump worked, kind of. But it's encrypted up the wazoo. Deep tech. Chances are they've added extra security to their system to stop this kind of attack. It's basically gibberish.'

'What about the bug?'

'Nothing but static.'

'That settles it. They knew, and they wiped the data. Spotted the breach and hustled me out of the building. They couldn't be sure if they could kill me without repercussions. But they'll be coming after me, and my family.'

'You don't know that,' Findlay said. 'It's every bit as likely they've upped their security, and the bug glitched. Or they added an ambient noise scrambler to their executive suites. And this isn't the kind of tech you just drop. This was already there. These are seriously paranoid people, Lois.'

'That's what has me so worried.'

He laughed. 'You should do well there, at least. You're as paranoid as they are.'

'They're not going to offer me a job, Findlay. They think I'm a goddamned spy. I am a goddamned spy.'

Findlay tapped his pad, chuckling.

'What?'

'They've offered you the job.'

'What?' She leaned in to read his pad, where a mail had come through from Sunset HR asking if the fake agency could convey to Lois that they would like her to start in two days' time. 'No way.'

'Way.'

'It's a trap. It's got to be.'

Findlay leaned back in his chair. 'It's a distinct possibility.'

'I mean it, Findlay, get my family out of here.'

He sighed. 'If you want to discuss it with Marisa, go ahead. But if they get whisked out of there by a black pod with no windows, it's going to look dodgy as fuck.'

'Okay, so... what? What do I do?'

'You go to work.'

She stared at the offer of employment again, squinting as though it might reveal some hidden meaning or truth behind the banal words, but they stayed the same. 'Right.'

Chapter Three

The next morning's breakfast was a reserved affair, the crew keeping their thoughts about the upcoming mission to themselves. Wyn tapped her pen idly on her pad as she ate powdered eggs that were neither powdered nor eggs, her eyes never leaving the real-time stats of their exact location. One hour until the last push. Her heart thumped a consistent rhythm with the pen.

Eggs finished, she crossed to the coffee station. She was going to need a lot of coffee. Her simulations had the whole thing clocking in at over five hours, closer to six, during which she'd barely be able to take her hands off the throttle, let alone fix herself a fresh cup. Besides, if she was in the suit, toilet breaks wouldn't be a problem, so she could go wild with the coffee. She picked up a large flask, meant for carrying water. If they hadn't packed it they didn't need it, so she took it to the machine, attached the nozzle, and kept hitting serve until the machine made a funny sound.

'Listen up,' the Captain said, entering the mess. 'Sunset want us to record a vid before we get going. We've not given them anything worth broadcasting in weeks, and they want to let the public know we're on course.'

A collective groan went around the crew.

'You know,' Wyn said, backing toward the door, 'I'd love to, you know I would. But I should do the last bits of prep.'

'Boooo,' Barnes said. 'No way should she get out of it.'

'Wyn's excused,' the Captain said. 'The rest of you, suit up. Be back here in ten minutes.'

Wyn poked her tongue out at Barnes, who shook his head in mock consternation at the desperate unfairness. Messages to Earth were the one thing they all hated doing. They'd signed NDA's when they'd signed up, their families too. Mission control limited personal calls to once a month, and they had to do a monthly crew update for the news feeds back home. Wyn's Baba told her the news feeds weren't even covering them anymore.

She thought about Baba. They'd not managed a call last month, so he'd be watching the news vids to see her, and she wouldn't be there. There was a stab of guilt, but she pushed it back down. She'd speak to him on the way home. There was too much anticipation in their conversations, too much fear from him. She was the last of them, and he didn't want to lose her. Pretty hard to diffuse any of that over the distance between them, especially when you knew several agencies were watching the call.

When she'd signed up to the mission, she'd expected an un-ending media spectacle, like the Juno missions faced before it. But the Minos crew weren't the most collectively interesting bunch of people to watch for the best part of a decade. It made sense nobody watched this shit back home—even the hardiest space nut would struggle to watch her siting in a flight module doing maths for years on end.

Coffee in one hand, pad in the other, she scooted through to the flight deck. Letting her pad drift, she swung open the lock and pulled the heavy door open. Bringing her feet up, she levered herself in, grabbing the floating pad once more as she went. She pulled herself into her chair. The vat of coffee wedged into the gap next to her seat; it even had a nice straw reaching up to her sitting position.

'How are we doing, Miles, me old mucker?'

'Within parameters, Commander.'

'Hold off on the sexy talk there, fast mover.'

'I'm afraid I can't yet discern whether you're flirting with me or making a joke.'

'Probably for the best. So, are we going to get through this?'

'The statistical analysis I have run in the last hour shows the odds are in your favour. Might I note you need to get into your flight suit, as per your discussions in the cargo bay?'

'You are a busybody, has anyone ever told you?'

'I can hear communications in every part of the ship.'

'Yeah, okay.'

Having gotten comfortable, she unstrapped herself with a sigh and took the cumbersome flight suit out from its locker. She hadn't worn it in over two months, the last time Ermine ran a safety drill in the middle of the night. Wyn prided herself on being one of the first to get into her suit, but she was an Air Force girl amongst a bunch of mechanics and science nerds. She'd been pleased to beat the Captain to the punch, though, though it didn't seem to faze him.

Changing in the cramped flight deck was less than ideal. Next to the Andy, the suits were the most technologically advanced items on the ship. Heavy, made of metal, but a polymorphic design that moulded itself to its wearer like a second skin. Hooking her legs into the suit, she pushed them down through smooth steel until they hit the boots, which gripped her feet like falling into quicksand. Once the feet were in, she didn't have long to get her arms into their sleeves as the suit tightened around her. It allowed for total flexibility of movement, but it was an inescapably weird sensation, especially once it started making micro-calibrations for her movement and breathing.

She took the helmet and placed it by the door; she shouldn't need it until it was time to head to the Andy, and the damn thing made her feel anxious when she wore it indoors. Flexing her hands within her gloves, she allowed the metal fabric to learn her movements and free her to make normal gestures. She'd need full dexterity.

Strapping herself in, she checked every screen except the main viewer. Close to the threshold. She ran through a last set of checks. Finally, she allowed herself to see past the screens, looking directly out of the cockpit to the planet beyond.

The scale and size of the planet gave birth to a horrific optical illusion—for a second it seemed they were inches away from crashing into its awful, swirling surface. She grabbed the throttle, about to pull the Minos away, before her conscious mind caught up with her terrified subconscious. She relaxed her grip.

Jesus, but it was big. The ever-shifting surface filled the entirety of Wyn's field of vision, the gases and storms on the surface broiling so fiercely they looked like they could reach out and grab her.

'Can I join you?' a voice whispered behind her ear.

She jumped in her seat and let out a startled cry. 'Jesus fucking Christ, Captain,' she said.

Captain Davis stood beside her, chuckling away. 'Sorry,' he laughed. 'Couldn't help myself. Hell of a view.'

His figure-hugging flight suit showed what good shape the old man was in. Damn, he was handsome for an old white dude. Shame he was married. Even if he wasn't, Wyn imagined Stef would be the one the Captain would show an interest in. Wyn doubted she'd get a look in. Not that she wanted to.

That was a confusing thought.

'Care to join me?' she asked.

'Well,' he said, moving into the second seat, removing several astronomical charts and pads of calculations. 'I am the Captain.'

'Good point.'

He began checking instruments. 'Sorry,' he said, when he saw Wyn watching. 'Force of habit.'

She smiled. Captain Davis spent many years sitting in her chair before taking the big job. He understood, better than captains past, the way to get the best out of your pilot was to get the hell out of their way and leave them alone. Trust in them and don't backseat drive. It was a refreshing change, and one reason she liked the man so much.

'We set?' he asked.

'We are,' she replied.

He nodded and looked back out of the window. 'It's a bit...'

'Terrifying?'

'That's the word.'

Wyn knocked a few switches, and the screen overlaid with vectors and ever shifting figures. In the top right was a countdown clock. Three minutes. Wyn's heart beat a little faster, even though she'd known how close they were. 'You want to say something to the crew?'

He nodded. 'Computer, patch me through to the main comms.'

'Yes, sir,' came a stilted reply.

A squawk of static announced him, and he sat up in his chair. 'This is the Captain. Everyone to brace positions, please. And strap in, it's about to get bumpy.'

He nodded to nobody in particular, and the speaker squawked again.

'Quite the speech,' Wyn said.

'Nobody wants to hear me rabbiting on. How are you feeling?'

'Not bad,' she lied. 'Want to get it done.'

She clicked a button on the dash. 'Li, Stef?'

'This is Li.'

'All set down there?'

'Good to go.'

She clicked the channel off. The counter above her head clicked into the last minute, and Wyn's hands moved freely over the console in a series of movements practised to the point of automation. She charged the boosters, released navigational control from the ship's computer, and added extra clamps around the exterior of the ship.

'Five,' she muttered under her breath.

'Four.' She took a breath and steadied her hands.

'Three.'

'Two.'

'One.'

She hit the booster at the same time as she grabbed the throttle, pulling it back and to the right, hard. For a moment there was a battle for the title of 'most horrific sound' between the protestations of the hull and the roar of the boosters. The force pinned Wyn back into her seat with such force the metal back of the chair pressed through the foam and into her spine. Abruptly the Minos jerked up and away from the planet, its huge red eye rolling back on itself as they moved clear.

The gravitational pull was so strong, trying to wrest control from it—even with two nuclear engines strapped to your arse—was far from easy.

'A little help?' Wyn said, struggling to get the words out. The Captain grabbed the co-pilot's stick. They put their collective strength into a turn up and to the right until they saw the curved horizon of the planet below them.

Checking the figures stationed around the screen in a flash, everything was where it should be. 'Okay,' she said. 'You ready?'

'Punch it?'

'Punch it. On three. Two. One.'

Captain Davis leaned forward and hit the second booster.

The force was even more intense than before.

Wyn tried to keep the joystick as calm as she could, her eyes never leaving the narrow vectors representing her flight path. The stick tried to wrestle itself from her grip. Pain burned through her fingers, and she let out a moan. Even a fractional misalignment at this stage and they'd overshoot Europa by a couple of thousand miles. Somehow, they remained within the corridor, until, finally, lactic acid burning through her forearms, she could ease off the thrusters.

She let out a lungful of air she hadn't even realised she'd been keeping hold of.

'Ready for the next stage?' she asked.

The Captain barely had a chance to respond with a choked 'ready' when Wyn pulled the stick around again, throwing the massive ship into a barrel roll. Wyn's stomach tried to make an escape attempt through her throat. She ignored it, and watched the horizon of Jupiter as it circled around, ending up above them. They were flying, for all intents and purposes, upside down, allowing them to be in the correct alignment for their approach to Europa.

So, where was she?

'Jesus, Wyn,' Captain Davis said. 'That was... that was fucking hardcore. I'm sweating like a glassblower's ass.'

She laughed, the tension creeping out of her system. 'Hold this course for a few hours, and we should find ourselves rocking up to an ice moon.'

Reaching forward, she grabbed the vat of coffee. It was still hot enough to catch in her throat. Exactly what she needed. Reaching forward, she flipped a switch and returned a semblance of control back to the ship's computer. The shuddering vibrations calmed until all was at a relative tranquillity.

'I'm glad we ended up with such an excellent pilot,' Captain Davis said, after a moment.

'Well, shucks, Captain.'

'I mean it. My biggest fear was flying with an unknown crew. It could have been a lot worse.'

She turned to him. He sat back in his chair, looking... different. Relaxed, somehow. Tired, too. She reached forward and picked up the vat of coffee, offering it to him. He waved it away.

'You knew Stef, at least.'

'True. But not knowing my XO, my pilot, my doc, my tech, half of my engineering team. I'd never experienced that.'

Wyn looked back out the window. There was a lot to do, but these were questions she'd wondered for the best part of half a decade, and the Captain had never been this open with her... shit, with anyone on the crew. 'How come you didn't use Commander Avenal? He'd been your pilot for years.'

'Grady was set to be my pilot on the Juno mission, back when this was a boat to Mars. We all were. All my usual crew. We were two weeks from launch, had worked on the project for two years already. Two years of intensive training and calculations. The Science team were in place. We had the ship's doctor who'd been a combat doctor for over two decades. Avenal and I had worked together for, shit, must have been fifteen years.'

'But the mission got canned.'

He nodded. 'We understood, of course. Once the floods took the east coast, we couldn't exactly take off from Canaveral anymore, but I assumed it was a delay, at best. Blinkered in my own little world. New York was gone. Washington. So many cities. So many dead. Government closed the doors to NASA about a week later.

'Grady quit. He was from New York. He moved back to help his family resettle. Iowa, I think. When Sunset started asking questions a few years later about this old bird sitting up in space, wasting away, someone mentioned my name.'

'That's how you ended up on the mission? I assumed you'd been there from the start.'

'No. I came on, it must have been six months into the planning. It was never my baby, not like the Juno mission. I tried to put the old team back together, but they weren't having it. I couldn't even pick my XO. Ermine was already in place when I joined.'

'Isn't that weird?'

He shrugged. 'He's an excellent XO. You lot may not like him, but he's a damn fine Airman. You forget he has the hardest job on the ship. He's a disciplinarian, so I don't have to be. Away from that, he's a good man. Me and him have had some fine talks, the two of us. He's a principled man. You should give him a chance.'

Wyn flicked a booster to slow burn as they briefly left the corridor of entry. Jupiter receded from their vision. 'If you say so,' she said.

'I do.' Captain Davis sighed. 'The only control they gave me was my pilot. I'm not going to sit here and tell you I didn't try to get Grady back on board, but as soon as I realised it wasn't happening, I knew there was only one choice.'

'So, why me?'

'You flew under Captain Hjunsou?'

'Yeah, doing shuttle runs up to the ISS.'

'We go way back.' He laughed. 'She would not shut up about you. Said you were the most capable pilot she'd ever seen. Better than Grady, even. When I saw your file, everything you'd been through to get where you were, I knew. No sense your talent wasting away ferrying billionaires about.'

Wyn looked at him, and couldn't stop a frown from forming on her face. Nearly four years she'd worked with Captain Davis, and she'd never known how she'd got this seat. It was bad form to ask why. She owed Captain Hjunsou a drink.

Or a slap.

'I hope I don't let you down, Captain.'

'I don't regret my decision for one second. Haven't since you stepped on board. And it's Jim.'

She nodded and gave him a smile. In the entire time she'd known him, she'd only ever heard Stef call the Captain by his first name. 'Okay. Jim.' She shifted in her seat and took another gulp of coffee.

The Captain leant forward, peering through the thick glass. 'Is that?'

'Yup.'

In the distance, barely perceptible at first, was a tiny disc of white.

Europa.

Win adjusted the screen, pulling the moon into sharp focus. It looked like a worn, scratched mint, something left at the bottom of the bowl at a restaurant, coated in the grubby urine-stained fingerprints of a thousand diners. She zoomed in, revealing deep red scars criss-crossing the surface, throwing the stark white of the surface into sharp relief.

'Ugly little motherfucker, isn't it?' she said.

'I dunno. I think it's kinda pretty. Like something my dogs would throw up.'

'You have a weird idea of pretty.'

They watched the moon in silence for a while, listening to the thrum of two nuclear bombs perpetually exploding away below them, hurtling them closer to the growing sphere.

'How we doing?' he asked, in a low voice, as Wyn worked the panels before her, adjusting a few inches every minute.

'This is the easy bit,' she replied. 'Get up close and put it in park. The moon has enough of its own gravity to hold her in orbit, but if I can work this right, I can set the Minos so it never gets exposed to the Magnetosphere.'

'I thought Li said she could take it?'

'If needs be, sure, but let's make doubly certain. I don't want to be halfway home when things fall apart.'

The Captain nodded. Wyn kept her focus on the panel rather than the approaching moon. The corridor grew thinner the closer she got. She might have called this the easy bit, but the slightest miscalculation and she'd blow right past the moon. Jupiter's hold was still strong—she skated along the edge of that hold, skimming it like a stone. Skim too hard and she'd lose the rotation, skim too shallow, and they'd sink.

'What the hell is that?' the Captain asked, leaning forward.

Wyn looked up. They were close enough to see the red marks and scars in the ice were not the same things. Red blossomed out from the cracks, covering flat ice, like blossoming red flowers.

'What we came for?'

'I guess so.'

'Only one way to find out.'

She powered the retro-boosters and killed the main engines, making the hull wail in discomfort once more, filling her ears with the rush of the engines. The flight deck rattled; for a second, she thought the ship might not make it.

Slowly, the Minos came to a halt. Wyn checked her instruments once more, made a few tiny adjustments, and gave one last booster thrust to kick them along the orbital path.

Unbuckling her seatbelt, she let go a sigh of relief. She stood, grabbing her helmet.

The tiny moon still glued Captain Davis to the screen.

'Hey,' she said to him, breaking the spell. 'You coming?'

Chapter Four

Lois's fears about her first day at Sunset didn't materialise at the front gate. Greeted by her new secretary rather than armed storm troopers, Neil—an affable, shy, and seemingly useless young man—took Lois to her office. A series of briefing notes lay spread out on various pads on a handsome oak desk.

'Carlos sent word that he'll leave you to become acquainted with these today, and he'll come by tomorrow to see how you're settling in and discuss your assignment,' he said in a whispered voice. He sounded utterly terrified at the prospect of Carlos being anywhere in the vicinity.

'Thanks,' she replied, giving him a smile she hoped conveyed both her gratitude and her desire to be alone.

He got the hint, giving an obsequious little bow before leaving.

The office wasn't bad. She was on the seventy-eighth floor. Curved glass overlooking the city made up one wall. Discarding the tabs with her information packets on, she went to admire the view. She could make out her house from here.

She drifted back to her desk and picked up the first briefing note. It was an internal report on staffing numbers within Sunset and its many subsidiaries. She flicked through to some less salubrious subsidiaries which had made the feeds over the past few years: Nefir, an arms manufacturer caught up in sales to a Pan African militia that had been taking over Mar-blighted farmsteads at the barrel of a gun; Propane company Exir, tainted by a child smuggling and prostitution ring within its supply chain and logistics divisions last year. Neither were listed. Clearly Sunset ditched the toxic parts of their brands whenever they got a chance. No doubt only far enough that they could claim deniability.

Whatever Sardy and his handler had been onto was big—big enough to get them killed. But beyond that, she had not a clue without either of them to tell. Interpol knew nothing about their progress, which made Lois wonder exactly what the hell their mission was. Lois had never started a mission without knowing the crime. Some whiff of criminality that justified them being there. Sardy had apparently begun his mission with no such taste of where it would go. A fishing expedition with the biggest shark in the ocean.

They couldn't count on their tech to passively crawl the servers, so there was one remaining option—detective work. But all she had to go on was what they showed her, and there were only a few days to achieve what would likely take months under the best of circumstances.

What she had were these briefing books, so she should start there. Pulling out her chair, she began to read.

By the time Neil came back in with a sandwich for lunch, she was none the wiser. Well, she knew a lot more about the role Sunset hired her for, but caught no whiff of international-scale high crimes and misdemeanours.

The job itself was a fat-trimming exercise. Despite being richer than God Himself, Sunset's takings year-on-year had dipped by a measly nought-point-five percent in the last tax year, so of course they were trying to scale back their workforce without taking a hit to productivity. It was a shitty job, but she'd never get to the point of recommending people get fired. But while she was there people would look at her funny, and she'd likely not make friends inside the company, which hampered her ability to dig dirt.

There was a knock at the door. Lois looked up from her files, noticing as she did so Neil had brought a coffee so long ago it'd gone stone cold.

In the doorway, clearly unaccustomed to waiting for an invitation to any room, was the woman she'd seen at her interview.

'Come in,' Lois said, standing up. 'Mrs Burgess, I believe?'

'That's right,' she replied, crossing the room and taking the seat opposite Lois without prompting, straightening her blouse as she sat.

'It's a pleasure to meet you,' Lois lied. In fact, her heart was pounding and her palms were slick with sweat. Thankfully, the head of security made no move to shake it. She took her own seat. 'How can I help you?'

'I wanted to touch base. I'm in charge of internal security, but I also have operational control of our security services. This is a busy time for us, and we're a growing part of the company overall. Obviously, with the work you're doing, I want to make sure we're on the same page.'

Lois wanted to laugh. Burgess wasn't here to threaten Lois, or pressure her, she was here to make sure Lois didn't cut fat from her part of the company.

'You want to ring fence security from efficiency measures?'

Burgess smiled. 'I'm sure there are plenty of efficiencies elsewhere.'

Lois nodded. 'As I'm sure you know, Carlos asked for a full root and branch review of the company, and he didn't mention any... exclusions. But I understand this comes in the middle of an interesting development for the security services. I obviously wouldn't want to impinge on that.'

Burgess tilted her head. Maybe she'd expected to intimidate Lois, maybe she'd expected an argument she could use to oust Lois before she'd even begun her work. She stared at Lois like a cat working out how quickest to kill its prey.

'You're aware of projects we have in the pipeline?' she asked, slowly, words chosen carefully.

'That depends.'

'On what?'

'On whether my information is complete. I guess that's up to you to inform me. Or not.'

'I see.'

Lois leaned back, trying to convey a relaxation far away from reality. 'Of course, there's no reason we can't work together to ensure I'm not stepping on your toes. How about this? Anything relating to your area I keep you looped in directly, and I don't make recommendations on Secure without running them by you first?'

'In exchange for?'

'Nothing. Seems the most sensible course.' She smiled at Burgess, pausing for a second. 'Well, there is one thing. These briefings give me a holistic picture of the company, but they're sanitised reports prepared by department heads looking to safeguard their own budgets. I don't doubt there's plenty of dead wood across the board. But if you could help me with proper access to the databases, I'm sure there are plenty of other areas where I could find efficiencies.'

Burgess smiled wider. 'If you have the right access?'

'Exactly.'

Burgess got up. 'Let me see what I can do.'

'I'd appreciate it.'

Burgess offered her hand. Lois took it, calm enough now that she didn't have to worry about a clammy grip.

'Oh,' Burgess said, releasing her hand and turning to the door. 'I understand you and your wife are local to the area?'

The hairs on the back of Lois's neck stood to sudden and alert attention. 'We are.'

Burgess turned back. 'We'll have to meet for dinner. I'm dying to meet her.'

'I'd love to.'

Burgess flashed one more smile and was gone, leaving Lois alone and unable to get her hackles down.

Still, she'd taken a step forward. Perhaps there was a way into Sunset's systems after all, enough to poke around. Aided by the security division, of all places.

So why did she feel like she'd sprung a trap?

Interlude

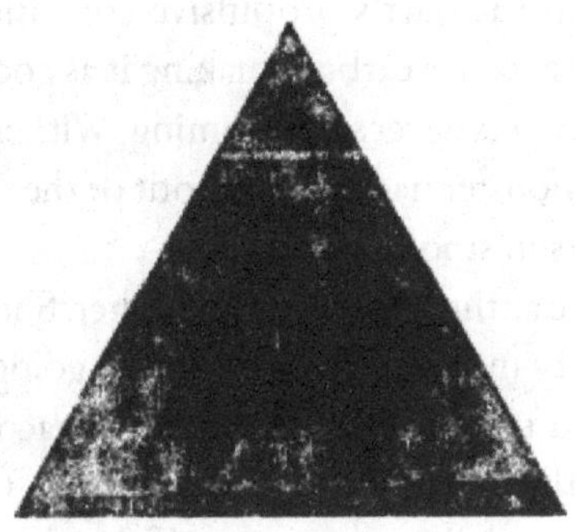

Near Poznań, Poland

June 2107

Asha wasn't like most other assassins. For one, she'd never been in the Army. Or Navy. Or Brownies. She went to Scouts once, but didn't like the whole 'being around other people' thing. People weren't her strong point. Up high in the mountains, she felt completely safe. Nobody could touch her, but she could touch anyone. Never met a mark she couldn't kill. Never missed.

She'd kind of fallen into the whole 'deadly assassin' thing quite by accident. She was a software engineer and model enthusiast, and those two things coalesced one day into a bit of a novel idea. Well, it wasn't a novel idea, exactly, but since the second Geneva Convention outlawed drone warfare fifty years earlier—joined in its banishment a few years later by AI—warfare had gone back to a distinctly face-to-face affair. Well, long-range rifleman to face, at any rate.

Asha circumvented the drone law in her design, and went right up against the codes for AI, too. The result was a propulsive dart system wedded to an adaptive display, feeding into a VR screen. She sat up high in the mountains, put on the helmet, directed the dart, and controlled it through a synaptic interface. She buried the tech deep in the dart's propulsive core and wrapped the whole thing in reflective carbon, making it as good as invisible.

Most of her targets never saw it coming. Witnesses swore blind some invisible monster had swooped out of the skies and ripped through the person stood next to them.

Of course, the authorities knew about her. She'd tried to shop the tech to pretty much every government going at first. When that failed, she'd tried flogging it to the megacorps. Sunset Secure had been the closest—she suspected they took a look and reverse engineered their own version. If they had, they'd kept it under wraps. But when there were no buyers, she had bills to pay from building the damn thing in the first place—the reflective carbon skin on its own meant she had to refinance her Mum's house—she had to find other ways of getting the money back.

That was how it started, at least. Then she found she had a taste for it, and a surprising lack of scruples.

The target today was a standard job. Nothing too difficult to manage. Opposition leader for some pissant European country. The kind of place which still claimed relevance in a world moved beyond it. The hit would have precisely no impact on the world stage, but that didn't much matter to her. She wasn't in it for the glory, or the politics. She was in it for the money.

The mark was in the offices of the Socialist Party headquarters, a gorgeous old stone building with red flags billowing from every corner. Somewhere inside hid her mark. He knew about the hit, and he'd done all the things one normally did in such circumstances. Sadly, none of them would work.

She went in through the air duct, uncomfortable for a moment as her vision changed from flying across open skies to hurtling through a confined space. She eased down on the speed, conscious that a clatter in the ducts would draw attention.

Activating the heat map, she searched for signatures. The steps he took to protect himself would be his undoing. She looked for a room with heat signatures standing by the doors and the windows, probably with a single signature pacing up and down inside.

Quite who'd tipped him off she didn't know, but it wasn't a concern. The absolute worst thing that could happen would be losing the bolt. She'd trigger the self-destruct mechanism and load up the next one. Nobody could look at it long enough to trace the signal, and even if they did, they'd have to be better than her, which didn't seem likely.

After a frustrating few minutes, she found him. Locked room on the third floor. They'd turned off the air and sealed the ducts. That left the windows—reinforced glass—or a front door that looked like solid steel.

Damn. A panic room.

She took a deep breath. Okay, so not a cakewalk, but not impossible, either. This mark represented a decent sum of money, one of her best paydays, so it was only right she put the extra effort in. She checked the primary interface—battery should last at least another twenty hours—plenty of time. She would wait it out. Eventually someone would bring him food.

She put the dart into a steady hold above the air vent nearest the front door. As soon as it opened, she'd go in.

Somewhere in the distance, a glide flew overhead. Nothing to worry about. An hour passed in silence, her eyes never leaving the silhouette of the door in her visor.

It was tiring, keeping that level of concentration up. She'd done it before—some industry bigwig she'd had to wait out for two whole days on one of her early jobs. The bolt had needed recharging more frequently then—every time she went back she thought she'd missed her mark. Her patience paid off eventually;

he popped his head out and she splattered its contents over his floor.

Her mind wandered, the subconscious taking control of the bolt, her present mind able to roam a little more freely. She thought about the weird turns her life had taken. About the tests her parents had subjected her to as a little girl when they'd caught her pulling the wings off a dragonfly. She was curious about it, hadn't meant to hurt it. And even at a young age she didn't see how it differed from the billions of bugs slaughtered every day for the burgeoning 'reclaimed carbon' movement in haute cuisine.

The school shrink diagnosed her as 'on the sociopathic scale'. Probably why, when she couldn't sell her design, she used it herself. It reduced the risk factor to practically zero, so why not? She'd hoped to sell the patent for millions, but she'd already amassed more than that in a few years. Two more years, she could retire to a private island. Or she'd keep doing this. It was fun.

Not this bit, though. This bit was boring. She checked in with her subconscious and found the door still barred.

'Hey,' a voice called out from behind her.

She let out a yelp of panic, breaking the link with the bolt for a split second. She set it to autopilot with a blink and turned round, removing the visor.

An old man stood behind her, his clothes little more than a rough assortment of rags. The weather here was not warm, but he had the leathery look of someone who spent their days in the sun. He looked ancient, pushing a hundred years old. He flashed her a half-crazed smile, revealing a mouth half full of broken teeth.

'Yes?' she replied, wanting to get this interaction out of the way so she could put her visor back on. She felt that way about most human interactions.

'What are you doing up here, alone in the mountains?' he asked.

'Meditating,' she replied, and went to put her visor back on.

'With a mech visor on?' he replied, looking at her curiously. 'You come away to nature, then hide under that?'

'Uh, yeah,' she said. 'If you don't mind, I'd like to get back to it.'

She had no intention of harming the man—he was no threat, and nobody was paying—but she needed to get back to her kill scene.

She slid the visor back down and tried to get herself mentally back where she needed to be to take control of the bolt. It wasn't the easiest thing to do, her analogue system interfacing with a purely digital one. She ran through the exercises to calm her mind enough to pick it back up.

The old man tapped her on the shoulder. She ignored it.

'Excuse me,' he said, the sound battling against the earpiece picking up harried conversation miles away.

He tapped again.

Urgh.

She slid the visor back off. The man was between her and the view, grinning that inane grin.

'What?' she asked.

'What is it you're doing, miss?' the man asked. 'Because, technically, this is my property, and if you're doing anything illegal here, I'd rather you moved somewhere else.'

'Nothing illegal, I promise. It's a sensory device, it allows me to meditate in total peace, and when I'm done, I can take in the scenery and maintain the sense of wellbeing.'

'I see,' he said, stroking the long grey hairs tufting under the pulled skin of his chin. 'Well, I guess I can't argue.' He gestured around. 'This is a place of sanctuary. Of peace. So you have come to the right place.'

She offered him a tight smile. 'Thank you. Once I've done my meditation, I could bring you some supper?'

His wide smile widened even further. 'Lovely. I am in a little hut about half a mile up the trail.'

'Sure,' she said. 'If you don't mind...'

He stepped back, holding his hands up in acquiescence. 'Of course.'

She lifted the helmet once more.

'Except,' he said, rubbing his chin.

She sighed. The old man had talked himself out of dinner. He was close to talking himself out of life. She may not be a trained killer, but she could throw an old man off a mountain easy enough. 'What?'

'I watched you hike up here, and you messing around with some kind of equipment, something which you launched from here. What was it?'

'Okay, old man, that's enough,' she said. 'Stop nosing around. What I'm doing here is none of your business.'

'Is that right?' he said, lifting his arms up to the sky with a flourish, his rags fluttering in the mountain breeze. 'Because it looks to me an awful lot like you are using some expensive military grade technology, controlled through some kind of neural link.'

'Does it?' she replied. She'd had enough of this. He'd moved away so she couldn't shove him, but it wouldn't take much to get him over the precipice. She stood and faced him.

'It does, indeed. Tell me, who is paying you to take out the leader of the opposition in this esteemed country?'

She laughed. 'That's what you're going with?'

'Yes, Asha Goddard, that's what I'm going with.'

She stopped moving discreetly toward him.

How the hell did he know a dead name? Asha, sure, retinal scans tied her to that name. But Goddard? She left that behind a long time ago.

She left it with the first man she'd killed.

He chuckled.

'Who the fuck are you, old man?'

'I'm the man who's come to stop you.'

'How did you find me?'

He fished around in his rags. Something about his countenance shifted, slightly. He didn't look so old. The rags became a costume.

'I'm skilled at finding people.' He pulled out what he was looking for. A badge.

'Interpol?'

'One and the same. I'll take the helmet.'

'No.' She clutched it tight.

He laughed. 'Think you're still going to make your mark? Hate to tell you, but the job was a ruse. A way to get you up on this mountain.'

'What do you want?' She looked around desperately for an escape, but the only way out was headfirst down the side of a mountain. Given the alternatives, it might not be the worst idea.

'Your helmet. Then for you to stop killing people. You've had quite the destabilising effect on a world that's already pretty unstable. We'd quite like you to stop.'

'What happens to me?'

'Depends on you. I can take you in, get you in front of an Interpol judge within about twelve hours. Be in prison in another six. Or you can come work for us.'

'Work for Interpol?'

'The pay's crap, compared to what you're used to. Oh, and we'll be taking whatever you've made so far, either way. Just FYI. Don't worry, we'll put it to good use.'

'You can't.'

'You know we can.'

She shook her head. 'What kind of work?'

'You come work for our coding team. No more bolt, sorry, but you've got a first class mind. You'll be working with a team.'

Tears welled in her eyes. So close. She'd been so close.

She shrugged. 'Not my scene.'

He reached forward, taking her arm in an adept move she barely had time to see. She stepped back, pulling away but losing her balance, toppling backward into the yawning expanse beyond the cliff face.

She was falling. Windmilling arms didn't help. Her stomach sank at the realisation that this was it. The end.

The old man's hand clamped on once more, pulling her forward, away from the edge. Her heart soared. She'd come so close to what she dealt out so often. She collapsed to the ground, making no attempt to escape as the Interpol agent pulled her arms behind her, cuffing her with metal cuffs that looked as old as him. Relief surged over her.

Perhaps she wasn't ready to die, after all.

Chapter Five

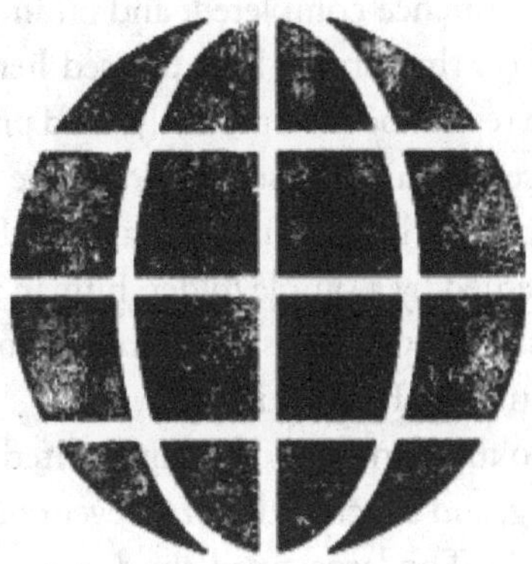

It came as a simple gift, wrapped in a box and topped with a bow. Lois took the box from Neil, who looked about ready to run to the corner of the room and throw up in the bin. She took the box and thanked him, but he was already halfway out of the room before she'd finished with the platitude.

'This should give you what you're looking for,' said the flourished handwriting on the tag, underneath which was a giant 'B'. Pen and paper. How ostentatious.

Inside sat a simple pad, its connectors removed, screen scratched around the edges.

What the hell was this?

She booted it up. An older generation, incapable of projections, isolated from its servers. It would also be impossible to hack or capture data from. As it loaded up, taking twice the time Lois would have imagined, she looked around her office. She was certainly being watched—standard business practice these days. Was Burgess watching Lois, waiting for her reaction?

Her first instinct was to call Findlay and arrange a meet, get this pad into the hands of the Interpol tech team. But that would be stupid. She couldn't rely on techies to find the smoking gun buried in here, if there was one. This could be a test, or a trap.

Nothing was what it seemed, and this pad was no different.

The loading sequence completed, and an image of a fingerprint appeared on the screen. Lois pressed her thumb to the screen, trying to remember when exactly she'd provided biometric data to Sunset to base this security on. The fingerprint dissolved, and a simple archive interface sprang up. Each of Sunset's divisions represented by a simple folder: human resources, security, pharmaceutical, operations, food, technology, head office, logistics, and sourcing. How mundane.

Using the lookup function, she highlighted a single folder entitled sourcing, and checked the size. Seventy-five exabytes.

What the fuck? The largest pad she'd ever come across had barely scratched a Petabyte. This was completely offline and held more data than she'd thought possible. Not bad for a beat up piece of shit that looked a decade old, at least. Who the hell had made this thing? Never mind getting this in the hands of Interpol's techs, she wanted to pull it apart herself to see how the hell it worked. It was like holding a data centre in her hands.

Apart from the impossibility of the device itself, why would Burgess hand this much data over? A cursory look into a few folders showed it to be a far deeper and more thorough version of the internal network she already had access to. Secret correspondence, memorandums, this had a log of every mail sent by every staff member. There were folders for things like Opposition Research—a euphemism for industrial espionage, lists of political donations, kompromat, and enough dirty deal information to bring governments down.

It was the motherlode.

It must be a trap.

For hours she dug through sub-folders, flicking through different topics, assessments, a million items of no relevance to anyone apart from those who'd committed them to type. Audio files, diaries, meeting minutes—it was overwhelming.

After the lights had gone out in the surrounding offices and the sky had bruised and darkened, she found what Burgess wanted her to find—an assessment of the entire Sunset global workforce to find inefficiencies. Created by HR a year earlier and kept secret because it would decimate the department that instigated it. But this was exactly what she needed to do the job they had hired her for. Wrapped up in a neat little bow and sat high up enough in a sub-folder that Burgess must have put it there for her to find. She might as well have walked into Lois's office and handed her the file directly and told her to pack her things.

Burgess didn't think Lois was a spy. She thought she was a threat, one to be moved along as quickly as possible.

Lois needed advice. How best to play this? She should speak to Findlay, get his... Shit. It was nearly eleven at night and she'd completely forgotten to check in with Findlay, or Marisa. They'd both be livid. Two people terrified about what might happen to her, and she'd forgotten them.

As if on cue, her wrist flashed with an incoming call alert, unknown ID. She tapped the alert.

'Hello?'

'Hi there, this is Prestige, calling about the flower delivery you have scheduled for next week. Can you confirm if Monday is still okay for you?' It was a woman's voice, no doubt in an office somewhere in Europe, but with a flawless midwestern drawl.

'Actually, can you make it Tuesday?' Lois replied. 'It'll be my wife taking delivery.'

'Sure,' the voice replied. 'Two PM?'

'Perfect.'

'Okay, thanks for shopping Prestige. You have a pleasant evening.'

The voice clicked off, and Lois smiled at the thought of Findlay sitting on the other side of the city, sighing an enormous sigh of relief. She'd even set up a meet.

'Flowers, eh?' a voice said

Lois jumped. She'd not even heard Burgess approaching.

'Need to apologise for these late nights,' Lois replied.

Burgess nodded. 'You got my gift?'

'I did. It's... comprehensive.'

'Good. You find anything useful?'

She smiled. She knew Lois had. That meant Burgess could follow what actions she took on the pad. How, if it had no connections? But of course, there'd be a camera on her. Lois gave a curt smile. 'A few things. One report in particular, but I'd need to investigate it properly to see if I agree with its conclusions.'

'Absolutely. I hope you don't mind, but I'd rather that...' she pointed at the black box, 'didn't leave the premises.'

'Of course.'

Burgess smiled and left Lois alone.

Lois stared at the doorway for a moment, deep in thought, and tapped her wrist once more. It buzzed.

'Lois?' Marisa answered. 'Everything okay?'

'Yep, sorry for being so late.'

'That's okay. I was beginning to worry.'

'Nothing to worry about. You get the girls off to bed?'

'Yep, just going myself.'

'Okay. Don't wait up, I might grab some food on the way back.'

'Sure.'

Lois waited a moment. 'I love you.'

'Love you too.'

The line cut. Lois stared at the dark doorway, trying to work out the next move.

Chapter Six

They made it through the cargo hold in less than five minutes, Wyn finally mastering the art of moving at speed in zero gravity—more or less. The Captain overtook her, his own technique flawless compared to hers. He opened the hatch to the cargo hold. The Andy, stocked and ready to go, stood in the centre of the empty bay, suspended by a lock holding it in place half a metre above enormous doors which would swing open, leaving nothing beneath but space and the moon below.

At their appearance, a heavy door opened, revealing the distinct shape of Stef on the other side, her suit shining in the cargo bay's stark lighting. Wyn and the Captain floated across the bay, grabbed the sides of the door, and eased themselves inside.

'We all set?' Stef's voice crackled in Wyn's ear.

'All set,' the Captain replied. 'Zoe, I have a hunch you're going to like it down there.'

Wyn ignored them, heading through the body of the ship until she got to the cramped cockpit. If the flight deck on the

Minos was small, this was like trying to pilot from inside an airing cupboard. She strapped herself into her seat and started the ignition procedure.

'If anyone's not strapped in by the time I've opened these bay doors, they're going to find out what it's like to be a pea in a can,' she said.

Nobody protested, so she tightened her straps and flicked up a rather dangerous looking red switch. Outside the cockpit, red lights flashed.

'How's it looking, Miles?' she asked.

'Systems are operational, Commander.'

'Have you transferred yourself over to the Andy's CPU?' she asked.

'Yes, Commander. We are good to initiate countdown.'

She flicked the red switch once more. Warning bells pealed through the cargo bay. A tiny clock on the dash counted backward from five.

Four.

Three.

Two.

One.

The doors opened, sucking the atmosphere within the cargo bay into the void. The Andy swung violently back and forth in its cradle. Wyn peered down. The white and red of the moon's surface sped by through the open doors.

'What the fuck is that?' Barnes cried through her earpiece.

'Computer, isolate comms channels to myself and the Captain.'

Barnes's protestations cut off.

'Captain?'

'Ready, Commander.'

Wyn reached forward and released the Andy from its mooring.

The Andy dropped like a stone, the open cargo bay doors rushing by in a blur. She forced her eyes to remain open so she could watch the rate of descent.

She waited.

Waited.

Waited....

She fired the boosters.

They didn't fire.

She tried them again, but nothing happened. At this rate, they'd crash into the ice with such force they'd explode on impact.

Shit.

'Computer, give me Stef and Li Wei.'

'Yes, Commander.'

'Guys, we've got no power to the boosters,' she said.

'What?' came the unified and somewhat unhelpful response.

She stared at her instrument panel, trying to work out the cause. She'd done the start-up sequences correctly, but the board sat static and unyielding.

The Andy began to tailspin, with no other forces to counteract it. Wyn's stomach leapt into her throat, and she grabbed the joystick out of sheer reflex, but it flopped around lifelessly without a navigation system to direct.

Thirty seconds, and they'd be dead.

Fuck it.

She clicked the master fuse to the main board, plunging everything into darkness. Every system onboard went dead together.

The system took a moment to reboot. Too long. The status bar crawled painfully slowly, a cube spinning endlessly until the monitor flashed with a ready command.

There was no time for booting sequences—there was a death spiral or a lunge skyward.

She hit the boosters again.

Force slammed her back into her seat. Grabbing the stick, she pulled up. Every muscle in her arms screamed at the effort, and she couldn't help but scream along with them. The fast approaching ice rushed beneath, and the Andy pulled upwards, toward the sky.

She pulled herself forward, the effort straining every muscle she had. 'Release successful,' she said to nobody in particular, the air struggling to make it out of her mouth. 'Boosters fired.'

The ship's computer brought up the topographical scanner, overlaying the deep red scars across the moon's surface with calm green lines and ice depth analysis.

'Miles, do you see a good option?' she asked, before realising the reboot could have fried Miles. He could be dead, and she'd not given it a moment's thought. Her stomach sank.

'Grid 24-c looks optimal,' he replied, as though nothing terrifying had happened.

She let out a sigh of relief.

The screen zoomed in, revealing a perfect patch of ice. Relatively smooth terrain, but close enough to a sizeable fissure. Grabbing the joystick, she yanked hard to the left, and made a hard circle back around. The nav computer calculated her best angle of descent, but she flipped it off. She'd do this by sight.

'Computer, patch me through to the crew.'

A buzz sounded.

'Guys, we're in for a bit of a drop, in case you thought we're crashing. It's going to feel like it.'

'That's a great comfort, thanks,' Barnes said, weakly. 'I already thought we were.'

'Everything okay up...' Stef started to ask.

'Comms off.' The line cut dead. She didn't have time.

She surveyed the moon. There was nothing below but ice and red. She didn't have time to compute what the hell the latter was, but she'd try not to land directly on it, if she could. She didn't want the first contact with an alien life form being to burn it to death with her thrusters.

Another deep breath, and she eased the stick down, sending the Andy into another tailspin, albeit one where she was nominally in control. Her stomach lurched, and she struggled to keep her breath regular.

'Hull integrity down ten percent,' the ship's computer told her in its disinterested voice.

Ice rushed up to meet her. Thirty thousand feet.

Twenty.

Ten.

Nine.

Eight.

She pulled the stick up, hard, and hit the thrusters. The hull squealed. Bile scorched the back of her throat, and her arms burned as she battled to keep the joystick in check. A growl of grim determination bubbled up in her throat, and the Andy came back under her control, righting itself so the ice was underneath again, the Andy's thrusters pointing down toward it.

Hitting a button on the dash, the screen filled with a view of the landing spot. It was perfect, with no red, and no angry scars in the ice. A nice field of white.

She fired the landing boosters, easing the Andy down slowly. The intensity of the boosters built as the ground approached until they hovered a few feet above the surface. She extended the landing gear from the sides. Finally, the Andy touched down with a hard jolt. Steam rose past Wyn's window as the ice reacted to the sudden appearance of red hot engines.

Panting, Wyn tried to regain her breath, skin covered in sweat, arms trembling. She peered up at the night sky. The Minos gleamed in Jupiter's light.

'Open comms,' she said, breathlessly. 'We made it. We've landed.'

Loud whoops and hollers rang across the comms, and she smiled. Somewhere under the roar of congratulations, someone dry heaved.

'Good work, Commander,' the Captain said, his voice cutting through the din. 'Come down and join the rest of us. Everyone else, you're up. Stef, Li, get the Tracker ready. Hamza, let's run a full diagnostic of the Andy. Zoe, let's get you out on the ice to look around, see what we're dealing with.'

Wyn let out a deep sigh. She'd done it. Anything else was going home, and that would be a hell of a lot easier.

'Miles, how long until magnetosphere threshold?'

'Seven hours, thirty-seven minutes, and thirteen seconds.'

She descended from the flight deck, legs trying to adjust to this new half-gravity. The crew busied themselves with tasks. Each took a few seconds to congratulate Wyn, or in Hamza's case give her a bear hug. The two congratulations conspicuous by their absence were Barnes—too busy trying not to throw up inside his helmet—and Ermine, who didn't bother.

For years she'd had nothing more to think about than getting these people down to the surface of this moon. It was now up to the rest of them to do their work. She'd been so singularly focused on her task, it hadn't occurred to her what she might do with herself afterward. She was like a parent outside their kid's birthday party, waiting for it to be over so they could give everyone a lift back home.

She could take a little holiday out on the ice. Set up a sun-lounger, bask in the glow of a gas giant. Letting out a heavy breath, the enormity of what she'd done swept over her, and tears welled in her eyes. She'd done it.

'Wyn,' the Captain said. 'Zoe is going out on the ice. Go with her, she's going to need some help carrying out her sample cases.'

'Me?' Approximately seventeen seconds into being a lady of leisure, and she already had a job to do.

'Don't you fancy being one of the two first human beings to walk on the moon of a different planet?'

Wyn shrugged. 'I suppose.'

Captain Davis gave her a pat on the shoulder and moved over to help Li and Stef. Zoe struggled toward her, arms full of boxes.

'Can you carry these?' she asked, handing them to Wyn before she could protest.

'Um, sure.'

'Come on,' Zoe said, 'Let's go.'

They walked to the doors to the cargo bay, which opened in a hiss of hydraulics, revealing a ladder down to the surface, surrounded by the cooling thrusters.

'So,' Wyn asked. 'What are we doing?'

'You mean besides being the first two humans...'

'I got the pep talk already. I mean, what do you need me to do?'

'Carry those boxes. Sorry, not exactly a glamour job.'

'From taxi to delivery girl,' Wyn said. 'It's fine. I'm glad to be of help.'

'Once we get out on the ice, I've got to find some kind of specimen of the organic compounds picked up by the probe. Once I've done that, I can use equipment here on the Andy to do some initial analysis before we go under the ice.'

'You think the red shit we saw on the way in is what you're looking for?'

'Makes sense.'

'Any theories about what it is?'

'Thousands. I can't wait to get my hands on it. You ready?'

'You two be careful down there,' Captain Davis said. 'Any sign of trouble, you get your asses back up here, okay?'

'Will do,' Zoe said.

The way down the ladder was difficult with arms full of boxes. 'Computer, are you recording this?' she asked.

'Affirmative.'

'I'd better make sure I don't slip on the ice and fall on my arse, then,' Wyn said, under her breath.

'Probably for the best,' Zoe agreed.

Wyn put her boot down on the ice and set the boxes down. She looked out across the expanse of ice and gasped.

Chapter Seven

Atlanta was a dull city. The charm the place held a hundred years ago was gone; the cultural heritage and the diversity of its inhabitants eroded by the presence of Sunset at its heart, bleaching it from the centre out. It didn't matter if you were black, white, or Hispanic. You lived in Atlanta, you were Sunset. Corporate blandness had washed all trace of the old city away.

There were no dive bars, no clubs, no dodgy areas, no wrong side of the tracks. None of the big tours rolled through Atlanta anymore, and none of its citizens even thought to dress outside of a colour palette of variations of beige.

It made clandestine gatherings of people with nefarious intent difficult to pull off. With all that lovely cover shunted out to the Glideports and surrounding towns, you were pretty much left with a series of bars and restaurants sharing the same well-lit decor to arrange a meet. You could walk into one bar on the east side of town and be magically transported to another on the east, and you'd only notice if the bartenders were different.

Lois slid into the booth at Bugburger at Twelfth and Oaks and waited for a server bot to come take her order. She had a few minutes—they always gave you an algorithmically calculated length of time to ponder your order before coming over. The place was busy; she took the last booth. No sign of Findlay at the other tables. She checked her watch. She was on time.

She looked over her menu, realising she actually was hungry. One of the other booths cleared just in time for Findlay's arrival. A server bot showed him to the new booth. Dressed suavely, but not so much as to stick out, he looked like any other businessman in town on Sunset business stopping for a bite to eat on his way home. He sat and looked over his menu, even though she knew the fake chicken was the only thing on the menu that didn't turn his stomach. She could barely stomach any of it, but there was a vaguely edible burrito she could order.

Looking around at the other patrons of Bugburger, she wondered what in the hell possessed them to come here on a Wednesday night. The food was abysmal, as it was pretty much anywhere, and yet here were people willing to splash out silly chits to get food they could easily print out at home.

Sunset was a leading name in reclaimed carbon—hell, it was a leading name in pretty much everything—even though everyone knew their recipes were the worst. Their home printers only printed their own recipes, so if you got hooked into one of the cheaper base units, you were stuck eating their swill until you could afford to upgrade. Restaurant chains like Bugburger were also hooked into exclusivity deals, meaning they charged customers for the same sub-standard crap they ate at home. So why the hell drove these people to a brightly lit box to pay three times as much for it?

Of course, the answer was social interaction. The importance of being seen. In a city this driven by The Company, these people were still working, late into the night. Networking.

Across the room, Findlay made his move as the server trundled over to Lois.

'Good evening, Miss,' the server bleated from its squawk box. 'Can I take your order?'

Findlay got up from his booth and made his way to the restrooms. As he drew close to Lois's table, he nudged the server. It toppled forward onto Lois's table, its metal facade slamming into the plastic table, splitting it in two. Findlay followed it down, as though pulled down by the metal server bot, until chaos enveloped all three.

'Oh my God,' Lois shouted, wincing in pain as the machine connected with her arm. That was going to bruise.

Everyone in the restaurant got to their feet, rushing to help. Several patrons worked to lift the metal server. Lois let out a howl of pain, as did Findlay.

'I'm so sorry,' he said.

A tiny, balding white man appeared from nowhere, a smear of black bug goo across his otherwise pristine white smock. 'Oh my word,' he said, practically sweating the words out. 'Are you both okay?'

'My fault, entirely,' Findlay replied, getting to his feet with the aid of two women from the booth next to Lois's. 'I slipped on something, I think. Miss,' he said to Lois. 'Are you okay?'

'I... I think so,' Lois replied, nursing her arm. It genuinely hurt, and she was dimly aware of a pain above her eye, the sensation of swelling. Shit. How the hell would she explain that tomorrow at work? Or to Marisa, for that matter?

'I'll call an ambulance,' the little man said.

'No,' Lois countered. 'No. I'm fine. If I could take a moment.'

'Of course,' the man said. He helped Lois to her feet, and led her out to the back of the restaurant, toward the kitchens. Findlay followed on as two other staff appeared, lifting the robot out of harm's way.

He led them into a storeroom. Two cheap folding chairs stood either side of a thin metal table, a card game abandoned on its surface.

'Thanks,' Lois said with a smile. 'Could I get some water?'

'Of course,' the man replied, with a nervous grin, before disappearing.

Findlay looked at Lois with genuine concern. 'Shit, I didn't mean to actually hurt you.'

'Well mission definitely not accomplished,' she replied, hitting out at his shoulder with her good arm.

'Well, you have to sell it, darling,' he replied in a mock English accent. He motioned to the cards on the table between them. 'Think it's a safe bet there're no cameras in here.'

'Yeah,' Lois replied. 'I reckon that little guy is already offering free meals to his customers while mag-wiping his surveillance, too.'

'Probably.'

'Still, let's not do this play again, eh?'

'Sure. What's going on?'

Lois filled him in as quickly as possible. The meeting with Burgess, the appearance of the pad, and her discoveries on it so far.

'Sounds like an old Rack device,' he said. 'Don't let it fool you. They can still monitor it.' He frowned. 'Don't remove it. They could have you arrested for corporate espionage. It would be a few days before we'd be able to get you out, and we don't have time.'

'What do I do?'

'Use the file you've found as the basis for your own report, take a few days to compile it, and use the time you're cross referencing as an excuse to dig into the files.'

'If I find something, how do I get it out?'

He fished around inside his jacket, and pulled out a tiny box, handing it over. Inside was a contact lens, and a tiny chip. 'Wear the chip behind your ear. The flip side is flesh toned. There's no transmission, so it's not detectable. You need to get the chip to us yourself. There's no audio, so don't go thinking it's good for conversations. Unless you catch Christopher Sun murdering a boy scout, focus on what's on that pad. Scroll through as much of it as you can. It's got enough on there for a day, so tomorrow I'll have one placed in your door frame to wear the next day. Leave the old one in its place for collection. Deal?'

She nodded.

'How are you holding up?'

'I'm okay. Tired.'

'We're at the home stretch.'

The door opened, and the little man came back in. 'Miss, Mister,' he said, his arms outstretched. 'I'm so sorry. I'd like to offer both of you a meal on the house tonight, and our unreserved apology.'

'Nonsense,' Findlay said. 'No harm done. I'd like to reimburse you for the table, as this is my fault. I insist.'

The little man countered with his own apologies, and Findlay countered once more, while Lois eased herself out of the chair and out of the room. Arm aching, fingers closed around the tiny box, she headed home.

Chapter Eight

Her suit could withstand lethal levels of radiation and temperatures below the coldest known to man, but it didn't stop the shiver running down Wyn's spine. Her breath caught as her eyes adjusted to the brightness of the surface, the light reflecting off the crystals in the ice as though lit by a billion fairy lights, stretching off in every direction as far as the eye could see. It was almost too much to take, and she nearly dropped her boxes.

Zoe stepped out from under the shadow of the Andy first, boots crunching on the ice below. Wyn followed, taking care to steady herself. She might have been joking before, but she didn't want to get home to find some vid of her falling on her arse repeating endlessly on the feeds.

'You think people back home are seeing this?' Zoe asked, staring out over the ice.

'I'm sure Sunset will package a nice little report for the press,' Wyn said. 'I doubt they'd let this go out live though. What if something went wrong?'

The surface wasn't as smooth as it first seemed. Cracks and fissures weaved across the ice, and what looked like rock formations jutted out from the ice everywhere, streaked through with red. Behind them, filling one half of the sky, Jupiter loomed; it looked close enough to reach out and touch. The complete absence of anything but space between, the endless white horizon, it sent Wyn's head spinning. She stumbled.

Zoe's hand clamped onto her shoulder. 'You okay?'

Wyn nodded, closed her eyes and took a deep breath. 'Come on,' she said, 'let's go find some of this red shit for you.'

'Deal.'

Moving awkwardly across the ice, Wyn focused on putting one foot in front of the other, trying not to get sucked into staring at the terrifying wonder of it.

She looked down at the ice and stopped. 'Zoe,' she called.

'What?'

In the light imprints Zoe's boots had left in the ice, red had blossomed, refracting along the crystallised surface like an inkblot.

'Oh! Bring my boxes over.'

Wyn waddled over with exaggerated steps, trying to see if the red had stuck to her own boots, but it was impossible to tell while carrying the boxes. She made it to the waiting scientist who took a crate and rested it on the ice.

'You can put the others down, too,' she said.

Wyn did as instructed and checked the soles of her boots. Flecks of wet red dusted them, but came off easily enough with a shake of the foot.

Zoe took a beaker from one case, and a spatula. She scraped some red from the ice and tipped it into the beaker. Holding it up to her visor, she peered inside.

'What the hell is it?' Wyn asked.

'Not sure yet,' Zoe replied. She shook the beaker and stared at the contents as though expecting it to do something, before placing it back into the box and snapping the lid shut. 'Come on. I want more samples.'

They trudged further from the ship, Wyn leaving two boxes behind and carrying the one already used. With the gravity about fifteen percent of Earth's, it weighed about as much as a piece of paper. They reached an outcrop of ice, its base thick with deep red.

Wyn could barely see where she was going, so when her boot came down on a patch of thick red which gave way under her, she stopped in horror.

'Shit, Zoe!'

'Stand still,' Zoe said. 'Don't put your foot down.'

Steam rose from the sole. Thick smoke, rising from both from her boot and the patch of red she'd stood in. 'Shit, Zo, please tell me this crap won't eat through my suit.'

She looked back to the Andy. It was a hell of a long way back. If it burned through her sole, there was no chance. Even if she crossed the distance before suffocating, she'd lose her leg to frostbite within seconds.

'Oh shit oh shit oh shit oh shit oh shit oh shit oh shit.'

'Calm down,' Zoe barked at her in a thoroughly uncalm manner. She steadied Wyn with her arm, taking care not to step in the muck. Wyn fought the urge to turn and sprint back to the ship with every fibre of her being. Zoe took the spatula and ran it along Wyn's sole, scraping off a thick red substance dripping from the blade like tar, into the waiting container. A thick globule of it fell to the ice, where it stopped steaming and formed a hard surface. Zoe put the first container into the crate and scraped the hardened red into another.

'What the fuck is it?' Wyn asked.

'I don't know, but it looks like it hasn't damaged your sole.'

Wyn looked back down at her foot. A few bits of gloop had indented into the grooves of the sole, but most of it had come off on the scalpel. It stopped steaming.

'We're going to need to think about decontamination protocols before we get back to the ship,' Zoe said. 'We don't know what effect exposure to this would have. I need to get an uncontaminated sample, too. Wait here.' She took out yet another sample box, and took some more samples, both of the red stuff on the ice, and the other, harder stuff. It was a good thirty seconds before Wyn realised she could put her foot back down.

'Are they going to be safe on board the Andy?' Wyn asked.

'Please,' Zoe scoffed. 'I've got so much isolation equipment on board that this gloop could take out a shotgun and aim it at our heads and we'd be fine. I'm more worried about the crap we've got on our boots.'

'Zoe, Wyn, come in,' Captain Davis's voice squawked in their ears.

'We're here, Captain,' Wyn replied.

'You'd better get back here,' he said.

Wyn peered back at the Andy, which seemed closer now she wasn't in fear for her life. The rest of the crew were out on the ice, standing around and looking at the ground.

'On our way.'

Zoe packed up the last of the samples, Wyn picked up the box and they trudged back. In the near-total lack of gravity, speed was not easily attained.

The crew stood around one of the Andy's struts, peering at it like people staring under the bonnet of a car trying to work out why it won't start.

'What's going on?' Zoe asked.

'Whatever this shit is, it's climbing up my ship,' Stef said. A thin trail of the lighter red substance had advanced a few inches up the strut.

'Jesus,' Wyn said.

'If it's made it that far in ten minutes it'll cover the ship by the time we're finished. We'll be stranded.'

'A little melodramatic, Hamza,' Captain Davis said.

'Is it causing corrosion or damage to the struts?' Ermine asked.

'Not so far,' Stef said, staring at her pad. 'Who knows what long-term exposure will do.'

'We have no idea what it'll do if it gets into the boosters,' Li said. He sucked air through his teeth to emphasise the point.

'I agree, it's not good,' the Captain said.

'Unless we're going to abort, right now, we need to make this work,' Ermine said. 'Suggestions?'

They stared at the red substance, collectively hoping that really, really wanting a solution might somehow will one into existence.

'What if we fired the boosters periodically?' Wyn asked. 'Might clear them out at least.'

'Maybe,' Stef said. 'Assuming fire would do anything to it.'

'They'd need to be fired on a cycle the entire time we're under the ice,' Hamza said. 'Someone would need to stay on board the Andy while the rest of us are under.'

'I'll do it,' Wyn said. She had no desire to be under the ice. 'I'm not needed down there. I can monitor the fuel ratios, too, make sure we keep enough to get off the ice again.'

Stef shook her head. 'No. The radiation shielding will protect from the worst of the magnetotail's effects, but not enough for such sustained exposure. You'd be dead by the time we got back.'

'Okay, not that,' Wyn said. 'What about Miles?'

'What about him?' Ermine asked.

'He can fire the engines on a cycle. He can monitor the fuel consumptions. Hell, he could probably pilot the whole damn mission back to Earth, if he had to.'

'Trying to talk yourself out of a job?' Li said.

'You want to fire me and let me put my feet up for the next few years, be my guest.'

'Hang on,' Barnes said. 'I like Miles, but are we sure we should trust it with something this important? I mean, it's Hamza's pet project, not a member of the crew.'

'Miles can do the job,' Hamza said. 'But it means he'd be staying up here on the Andy, not coming under the ice. I was planning on porting him over to the Haven's CPU to help with analysis, but this is more important.'

'Miles?' Captain Davis said. 'You up to the task?'

'I won't let you down, Captain,' Miles slurred.

'Li, Hamza, Stef, Ermine, you need to get drilling, sharpish. Zoe, you get to work on figuring out what the hell this shit is.'

'We need to work out a decontamination protocol, too.'

'Best get to work.'

The Tracker—a long snaking truck with tank treads—stood loaded with drilling equipment, and the Haven habitat they'd be taking under the ice. Li took the wheel, the others climbing on board wherever they could find space. Li fired the engine, and the Tracker trundled toward the crevice. Wyn, Barnes, Zoe, and the Captain remained.

'Zoe?' the Captain asked. 'Honestly, did you expect anything like this?'

'No.'

The Captain nodded. 'Okay. Let's get to work.'

Wyn stared out at the retreating Tracker as it wound its way across the ice into darkness, trying to shake the feeling that this moon held a few surprises yet.

Chapter Nine

By the time Lois got home, the bruise over her eye swelled to the point it impeded her vision, and she worried her arm might be broken. Of even greater concern was what Marisa would say when she saw the state she was in.

Steeling herself at the front door, she took a quick look at her compact and placed her hand on the scanner, wincing at the movement of her hurt arm.

'What the hell?' Marisa exclaimed, before Lois was even through the door.

'I can explain,' Lois said, crushingly tired and not in the mood to explain anything.

'Are you okay?'

'I'm fine. Honestly. This was Findlay. We had to engineer a way to get a private moment, and it went slightly wrong.'

Marisa led her into the living room. Candles burned and jazz played on the stereo. A book and a half-finished glass of wine sat on the table.

'You waiting up for me?' Lois asked.

Marisa sat Lois on the couch, holding her face between her palms, staring intently at the bruising on her wife's face. 'I spend my time worrying about you these days.' She got up and crossed to the kitchen. Lois sank into the couch, letting the tension of the day ease out as the soft leather claimed her. Marisa returned, an ice pack in one hand and a wineglass in another.

'Thanks,' Lois said, taking the first and pressing it to her eye before sipping long from the second.

'How worried do I need to be?' Marisa asked, sitting back down beside her.

'Should just be a few more days,' Lois replied. 'We're close, already.'

'Are you being safe?'

'As safe as I can. I still think you and the girls should get out of town.'

Marisa shook her head. 'I'm not doing anything to rouse suspicion, not with you in there. Besides, I need to be here when you get back each day. It's hard enough not knowing in the same city, let alone wherever the hell you're planning on sending me.'

Lois sighed. 'I know. But you giving the game away and not being here is far less scary than you being here and them deciding to take you, or the girls. I couldn't live with myself.'

Marisa stood up. 'How do you think I could live with myself if you get captured because of me?' She paced across the lounge. 'I hate this. I hate it. It's not fair, not on me, not on the girls, not on you.'

Lois grabbed her wife's hand, stopping the pace. 'I know,' she said, looking into hazel eyes welled with tears. 'A few days. We'll say my father is sick, that you're taking the girls to cheer him up. I mean, that's not even a lie. They'd love to see him. And it's only a short glide away. I'll send word to Findlay to make sure you get on the glide, see about protection at the other end. Yeah? I promise you, I will contact you every day.'

Marisa stared at the ceiling.

'Please,' Lois said. 'It's a few days. I'll join you as soon as this is over, and we'll fly off into the sunset.' She pulled Marisa's arms down, gently. Marisa acquiesced, landing gently on Lois's lap. Lois ran her hands through Marisa's hair and planted a kiss on a cheek still salty and wet from tears. 'I'm sorry,' she whispered. 'It'll be over soon.'

Chapter Ten

Wyn and Zoe set up a decontamination protocol inside the Andy, a task made unnecessarily cumbersome by having to do it in suits themselves in need of decontamination. They set up a chemical shower inside the cargo bay and rigged up a seal around it so anyone coming in or out would need to pass through.

Protocol achieved, Zoe disappeared with her samples to the miniature lab set up above the cargo bay, next to Barnes's medical bay. The Andy wasn't designed for much more than shuttling people to and from the Minos, so it didn't have a mess, or bunks.

Barnes followed her up the ladder, presumably so he could sit on his own and re-evaluate his poor life choices. That left Wyn and the Captain to prep the cargo bay to receive the collected materials.

The plan sounded simpler than the reality. Stef and the others would drill through the ice, the drill installing a wide pipe in its wake. Once they broke through the surface ice, the habitat—a spectacular feat of engineering—would shoot down the hole before expanding under the ice into working living quarters. Then the crew would descend. Once there, Zoe's role was to continue her work. Once the magnetotail passed, most of the crew would return to the surface and collect as much of the organic substance as possible. Since attempts to replicate the compound from data alone had failed, they'd need to collect as much as they could. Collect, analyse, get back to the habitat. Rinse and repeat in as few cycles of the magnetosphere as they could manage. All told, the operation could take up to three weeks.

Wyn and the Captain checked the tank and the pump that would extract the collected materials from the Tracker once it returned. They worked for a few hours, checking everything in silence, passing barely more than grunts to each other.

Ermine returned with the Tracker, having deposited the others at the drilling site. 'Looks like there's serious interference on the comms,' he grumbled. 'Couldn't reach you from the drill site.'

'Everything on track?'

'Stef and Li say initial drilling has gone fine.' He headed back up the ladder.

'Commander,' Miles said through Wyn's headset.

'What is it, Miles?' she replied, stowing away a heavy box.

'You are becoming dangerously dehydrated and are lacking in nutrients. I would advise you take a break.'

She sighed. 'Oh, yeah? Do you see a Quoffshop anywhere on this ice?'

'You have a rehydration tube inside your helmet which you can use to access both water and nutrients.'

She rolled her eyes. 'Stuff tastes like feet.'

'I'm going to have to insist, Commander.'

'Miles, I'm not sure where you get the authority to insist on anything.'

'If you'd like I can bring the Captain into this conversation?'

'Fine.' She took a big pull on the tube, filling her mouth with warm, chemical-tasting grimness. She winced as it hit the back of her throat. Some of the crew seemed to actively like this stuff, which reminded her of the awful nettle tea her nan used to make for her brother and her.

The memory of her brother rose, unbidden. The sight of his hand in hers as they peered through an open doorway, watching adults rush about in a panic. Laughing as the first trickles of water sped past their feet, splashing their shoes.

She shivered.

'You okay?' the Captain asked, appearing beside her.

'Fine. We set?'

'Just waiting for Barnes and Zoe before we head out to the fissure and join the others.'

'I'm ready,' Zoe said, reappearing in the cargo bay with more boxes, followed by Ermine. 'I want to get back out there,' she added. 'Get some more samples. What I'm seeing so far makes no sense.'

'What do you mean?' Wyn asked.

'It's too early to say for sure. I need to get under the ice, spend more time assessing. I've sent what I can to Sunset, maybe they'll have better luck.'

'Doctor Barnes,' Ermine called. 'You ready to leave?'

'Not yet,' Barnes called back. 'Sunset have asked for a full compile of crew assessments before we go under the ice. I'm going to be another hour at least.'

'Why don't we take this stuff out to the others, and I'll drive back and pick Barnes up,' Wyn said. 'We've still got time.'

'It'd be good to get out there,' Zoe said.

'Doc, you going to be okay on your own here?' Captain Davis asked.

'Sure,' Barnes replied.

'Let's get going.'

Wyn climbed on the back of the Tracker, perched behind the driver's cab. Ermine took the wheel, the Captain beside him. Zoe sat side-saddle on the edge. The engine rumbled, and they were off, moving slowly but methodically to the fissure. Wyn peered across the ice, trying to make out the others, but aside from a vague electric glow on the edge of the horizon there was nothing to see.

She turned back, resting her gaze on Jupiter, watching the enormous eye as it watched them back, implacable.

Something darted across the periphery of her vision.

'What was that?' she called, whipping her head round to where the movement had been.

'What is it?' the Captain asked.

Ermine slowed the Tracker to a halt.

Wyn strained, trying to unpick what she'd seen. Zoe joined her, staring out across the ice. Jagged shards rose from the surface. She was sure that was where the movement had been.

'I don't know,' she said. 'Something. Movement. I'm sure of it.'

'Your mind playing tricks on you,' Ermine said, haughtily. 'Let's keep going.'

'Miles, can you scan the area?' she asked.

There was a crackle before Miles's voice responded, distant and broken. 'Negative, Commander. I'm afraid the temperature makes scanning all but impossible.'

'Miles,' the Captain said. 'You're breaking up.'

'Yes, Captain. There's some... interfere... comms.'

'Okay,' Captain Davis said. 'Let's get going.'

As the Tracker pulled away again, Wyn kept her eyes glued to the jagged ice, watching for movement, until it was too far away to see.

A chill ran down her spine.

They drew closer to the others. Clouds of steam rose from the drill site, and heavy lights cast an odd shine across the ice.

The closer they got, the more they rode over the hardened red stuff which had made Wyn's boot steam. The tracker's tread burst pockets of it, releasing puffs of white smoke.

Ermine pulled up by the others. Stef stared into the fissure, a set of instruments in her hands. Hamza paced back and forth, leaning over and peering into the fissure every few seconds. Li sat in what looked like the booth to a crane, except this crane went straight into the ice.

'How's it going, Stef?' Captain Davis asked, as they disembarked from the Tracker.

'The fissure itself is stable, no sign of seismic activity, or cracks coming from our drilling. But it's as bad as we thought with the depth.'

'Will we make it through with enough time to get under the surface?'

Stef shrugged. 'Your guess is as good as mine.'

Captain Davis nodded. 'Keep working at it.'

'You seen anything strange out here?' Wyn asked.

'Aside from this red crap?' Hamza replied, wiping some off his boot.

'Aside from that.'

'Nothing. All quiet on the red-gloop front. Why, what have you guys seen?'

'Nothing,' Ermine said. 'Come on, let's get this stuff offloaded.'

They hauled boxes off the Tracker, and discovered the fast-moving red stuff gave them a logistical headache. They had to be strategic in where they set up to make sure their equipment didn't get covered in it, except there wasn't much safe ground around. Stef had taken to carrying a small acetylene torch around to burn it off as it grew. Still, at least she'd confirmed fire killed it.

Wyn's already tenuous grip on the concept of time abandoned her altogether. She had no idea how long they had until the magnetosphere would crest the horizon and fry them all. At least on the Minos, the ship's computer acclimatised their surroundings to a day/night schedule. On Europa the days lasted three and a half Earth days, and that was in rotation around Jupiter, not the sun. Their star was still visible, but compared with how it sat in the Earthen sky, it was little more than a night light. The surrounding light came from the ice, which reflected the light from Jupiter; one more disorientating thing about this place.

'Ssssk ** fffft,' came a squawk over their radios.

Everyone stopped what they were doing and looked to each other.

'Miles, what the hell was that?' Wyn asked.

Silence.

'Miles?' the Captain asked.

'...Barnes.... scanning...heartr...parameters...elevated...'

They turned their gazes back to where the Andy was, out of sight.

'Barnes, come in,' Hamza said, but there was nothing but static.

'Ermine, you stay here with Stef and Li and keep drilling. Hamza, Zoe, Wyn, you're with me.'

They ran back to the Tracker, or as best as they could manage. The Captain threw it into gear; the grips sliding on the ice for a moment before gaining traction, propelling them forward. They started back toward the Andy.

'Can you see anything?' the Captain called to Wyn and Hamza, perched atop the vehicle.

Wyn peered through the darkness, but there was nothing but endless ice.

'Miles?'

Nothing.

'Miles, can you read me?'

'Yes, commander,' Miles replied, his voice distant but clearer.

'What the hell is going on? Where's Barnes?'

'Doctor Barnes is no longer aboard.'

'Where the fuck is he?'

'I am reading him as outside the craft.'

'Ffttt **** p*p.'

'Barnes, can you read me?'

'I...' The voice cut out.

They were still a way off. Wyn peered through her visor, trying to get a sense of what the hell was going on back there. She could make out the tall bullet shape of the ship, but the way the Tracker bounced around the ice she couldn't see any more.

'Hang on, Barnes.'

A flash of movement, over to their right, far away from the Andy. Something moved across the ice.

'Over there!' she screamed, pointing.

'Holy crap,' Hamza said next to her. 'I see it. Captain, there's definitely something out there.'

'We've got to get back to the Andy,' the Captain replied. 'We can worry about that later. Ermine?'

'Yes, sir?' the XO's voice crackled, distant.

'Keep your eyes open, okay?'

'Sir? Sss....' The signal crackled and was gone.

'Shit.'

They approached the Andy at speed; the Captain skidding the last thirty feet on a combination of ice and brakes. Wyn and Hamza jumped clear as it came to a stop. Wyn looked around, searching for the doc, or anything else.

She saw him, propped up against a support strut, booted feet sticking out across the ice.

'Captain,' Wyn shouted, and they dashed over as one.

'He's unconscious,' Zoe said. She held her pad out, scanning him. 'We need to get him inside.'

'What about decontamination protocols?' the Captain asked.

'There's no time,' Zoe replied. 'His helmet visor's cracked. It could go at any moment. He'd be dead instantly.'

'Zo, protocol is protocol,' Hamza said. 'You'd risk the entire crew to save him?'

'You saying we should let him die?' Wyn asked.

'We don't know what's wrong with him,' Hamza said. 'I'm not trying to be difficult, but rules are rules.'

'I don't think the algae is dangerous,' Zoe said.

'Know that for a fact, do you?' Hamza replied.

'Enough,' Captain Davis replied.

'Yeah, cut it out, will you?' Barnes said, weakly. 'No need to break protocol for me.'

Wyn let out a long breath of relief.

'What the hell happened, Barnes?' Zoe asked. They brought the doc to the airlock, but no further.

'I saw something. I panicked.'

'What did you see?' Wyn asked.

Barnes coughed. 'You're going to think I've gone space crazy. We're not alone out here.'

Chapter Eleven

Walking up the long steps into the Sunset campus, Lois felt a spring in her step. Marisa and the girls left for the glide station an hour earlier; Findlay would meet them and ensure they made it safely to their destination. As for Lois, she had the contact film in place, and the storage chip. She would go in and spend the day looking through the rack pad, if she had to, until she found some dirt. Hell, she might even finish by nightfall. Could join the girls by tomorrow morning.

Neil greeted her in his normal, skittish way, terrified enough about bringing her a coffee, let alone discussing the day's agenda. As he ran through the few meetings on the books—department heads desperate to ensure their budgets remained intact, mostly—her mind wandered. As tempting as it was to blunderbuss through the day trying to gather information, she had to remember Burgess monitored everything.

No, the better way to play this was to call up the HR report, and start her own file mirroring it. Go through recommendations for each department in the HR report and use it to go through the rack for each department until she found the dirt she needed. This meant sifting through thousands of meaningless files. The dream of finishing today died as quick as it came.

'Thanks,' she said to Neil, once it became apparent by his nervous silence he'd stopped trying to talk to her. He turned and disappeared back to his office, and she unlocked the beaten rack pad from her desk, setting it on the desk and staring at it for a moment. She booted up her own pad and got to work.

After several hours of going through meaningless files on projects, noting the obvious inefficiencies in them, double checking them against the HR report and creating her own, she'd almost forgotten what she was doing there in the first place. That was until she came across the first potential smoking gun.

Snowstorm—a project in Canada trialling a set of coordinated vaccines in response to floods in the area. Floods meant water-borne diseases, and these leaking into the water table led to hundreds of thousands of deaths. Lois found an internal report detailing the truth of Sunset's involvement. They'd used the crisis to dump dangerous overstocked meds into the local water in areas where many were already dying. They caught a tidy windfall while escaping blame for the deaths their medications inflicted. What were a few thousand extra deaths when that many were dying every day?

There was no actual smoking gun in the documents, just reports by bewildered local agents wondering what was going on, why their efforts weren't working. If there was criminal intent there, it wasn't by the staff on the ground. Not unless you wanted to go after them for using hookers forced to turn tricks to feed their families in such a desperate situation.

Therein lay the problem. She wanted juice. Something huge, going right to the heart of Sunset as an organisation. She wouldn't find that in the personnel files of the grunts on the ground who likely had no idea what the Machiavellian master-strokes of their paymasters were.

The structure of the HR report wasn't helping much. If there was dirt in there, it was likely in the areas of Sunset's security forces. The one place she didn't dare tread. She'd all but promised Burgess she wouldn't. Part of her wanted to go in and search for Dan Sardy's name, try to find the file on him. There was bound to be one. Or would there? Would Burgess be that ballsy?

'Hi,' a timid voice came from the hallway. Lois looked up to see Neil hovering in the doorway.

'Come in,' Lois said.

'Thanks,' Neil replied, and came in, taking the seat opposite Lois. He'd never so much as lingered close enough to have a decent conversation. Now he sat at ease. Well, at ease might be the wrong term. Lois doubted that was a state Neil never actually achieved. 'I wanted to see how you are settling in, whether there was anything more you'd like me to be doing?'

'Um, well, it depends. What more would you like to be doing?'

'Whatever makes me useful to you. Your predecessor, for instance, had me running all sorts of additional research for him.'

Lois had to stifle a chuckle. She couldn't imagine throwing this poor man into the fray. Here, kid, try to unpick a massive criminal conspiracy, would you?

'I see. What kinds of strengths do you bring?'

'I'm not bad at digging through things, and I know the company pretty well. The players, the internal politics. I also have a route in through the PA's. There's not much we can't find for each other, given the right... motivation.'

Lois sat back, considering the young man anew. 'My predecessor?'

'Technically his title was different, but he was looking at the same efficiencies you are.'

'What happened to him? Could I pick his brains?'

He winced, then shook his head. 'I'm afraid that won't be possible.'

Sardy. It had to be.

'Well,' Lois said. 'Starting tomorrow, I'll have a few things for you to run down. In the meantime, thank you for your candour.'

Neil flashed a nervous smile and stood. He turned for the door but paused in the doorway, returning to his standard nervous persona. He looked as though he wanted to say something, but changed his mind. In the end, he opted for a timid 'good night,' and was out the door before Lois could return the farewell.

She turned back to the rack pad. It had been out on the desk the whole time. Shit.

She'd reached the part of the HR report dealing with scientific research and development departments—heavily targeted for cuts—so she wanted to at least take a surface look at them before calling it a night. At least she didn't have to worry about Marisa at home waiting for her.

Digging into the R&D files, it became clear how mammoth the task would be. The folder structure wasn't as clear as the others, with every project codenamed with titles like Sundown, Voice, Quell, Button, and thousands of others. None had further labels on them. Still, she did her best, flicking through folders at random, trying to find anything.

She didn't understand any of it—most of it seemed written in gibberish.

One folder was simply called Mar. She opened it out of curiosity and found over a hundred sub-folders. This wasn't surprising—Sunset were at the fore of the global fight against the disease which had brought the planet's farming industry to its knees. But alongside folders for the Sunset funded Minos mission, there were folders labelled 'pathogen' and 'HPP' and '21'. Each held hundreds of sub-folders, each archaically named.

It was late, and she wasn't getting anywhere. She'd stumbled into a folder in Chinese, staring at it in the hopes it would start making sense. Or, at least, that whoever ended up going through this shit back at Interpol might make sense of it. The files were text and financial statements, molecular drawings, schematics. There was a single image tagged to the bottom. A group photo—eight men and a woman at a barbecue. She closed the image down, but something pulled on the tendril of a memory, and she opened it up once again, leaning forward to look at the image closer on the battered screen.

One of the men was Christopher Sun, more relaxed than she remembered ever seeing him on the feeds. An old man, but one whose wealth had let him fight off the worst ravages of that age. He was handsome, well dressed, with the body of someone half his age. And yet, even with his wide smile here, the eyes looked dead, like a shark's. Next to him was Burgess. Carlos was there too, looking off camera as though his mind was somewhere else. Burgess beamed. There were four Chinese men, smiling, each with a beer in hand. Two more men off to the side, not looking like they were having as much fun. She recognised both, but couldn't place their faces.

In front of them, the reason for the smiles, a barbecue filled with enough real meat to feed a small village. Behind the eight, small children ran about, faces blurred by motion. The picture had been taken on some palatial estate. Could even be Sun's own palace, situated not far from where she sat.

Finally, it clicked. The two off to the side. The mission Captain, Jim something. And Ermine. Second in command of the ISS Minos mission.

She checked the date stamp. October first, twenty-one hundred and two. Four and a half years ago. Around the time the mission took off.

She closed the image. This felt significant somehow, but she couldn't tell why. Sunset had bankrolled the Minos mission with joint funding from the Chinese conglomerate. So why wouldn't they throw the crew a party? Except, where were the rest of the crew?

She searched for other images, but there was only one.

She checked her watch. Jesus, it was getting late. She should get home and make sure Marisa and the girls got to her father's safely. She could dig into this more tomorrow.

Locking the rack pad back in its drawer, she grabbed her coat and headed for the door.

The Atlanta air was cool on her face, the night still and quiet. There were no bars or restaurants by the headquarters, just long stone steps leading away from the towering spire toward the rest of the city. The link stop nearest the office was closed at this time of night, so Lois would have to walk half a kilometre into town—she might as well walk home. She started back, wondering if she should try Marisa, or wait until she got home. Probably best to wait, so they could talk at least relatively freely.

A few blocks away, lights flashed, red and blue cascading down the streets. Sunset security doing their sweeps, no doubt. Instinct had her checking the back streets, wondering whether to duck down one and try to slip by, but if someone already had eyes on her that'd look suspicious. Besides, she didn't have the rack pad, and there wasn't much they could pin on her unless they found the chip nestled behind her ear. If they knew about that, they'd have done something before she left the office.

She continued on, heading down the stone steps toward the city centre.

A crowd gathered near the lights, held back by police officers. Lois closed the gap, thinking she still might need to take a detour if this was a pod crash. Whatever it was, they'd closed the intersection.

Straining to see over the heads of the onlookers, simple morbid curiosity told her to see what was going on, rather than some profound intuition.

Once she saw the body, a sinking feeling took over.

In the middle of the street, half on the sidewalk, half in the road, his throat cut so viciously the wound reached his ear, his jaw severed by the force, lay Neil. His glassy eyes stared back at her, lifeless and black.

The story continues with
BLINDED BY LIGHT

Grab the next thrilling installment of the

SUNSET CHRONICLES

SCAN ME

Leave a review

I really hope you've enjoyed reading *Hanging Moon*.

If you did, the nicest thing you could do for me right now is to leave a review. Reviews are absolutely crucial to discoverability, and social proof. If you could take a second to rate and review this at the store of your choice, I'd hugely appreciate it.

Thanks,

Paul

Leave a review

Author's Note

Over the past few years, my teenage daughter has been getting more and more into horror, starting with the recent remake of It and spiralling from there. She's pretty hardy, and doesn't hide behind the sofa the way I used to at her age. I'd love to say that having a horror-loving father (and mother) has also influenced her, but that's really not the way parenthood seems to work. Either way, she's got a taste for scares, and that makes me just about as proud a parent as when she comes home with a glowing school report.

Recently we were talking about the scariest film we'd ever seen, and I answered with a reflexive invocation of The Exorcist and The Shining, but over the last few days the question has wormed its way into my skin and I've been thinking about the most terrorised a horror film has ever made me.

Candyman.

It's a scary film, but perhaps a little context here. I was raised by publicans, who worked every night. At a certain point I got old enough to be left without babysitters to fend for myself of an evening, and most days this led to a trip to the local purveyor of VHS tapes to get something that fulfilled one of two criteria: Fighting, or frightening. My parents were okay with me watching most things as long as they weren't full of rude bits (there was the time when I wanted to rent Red Heat only to be vetoed over the title, much to the consternation of a young man who just wanted to get his Arnie on).

At the time of this tale, we lived in a flat in Docklands, London, a place with amazing views over the Thames and a lounge blessed with a pretty sizeable television for the time. I'm sure if I showed it to my kids they'd laugh at its tiny proportions, curved screen and fat arse, but back then it was the height of televisual sophistication – the perfect place to sit down of an evening, for instance, and chill out with a tale of bees and hook-hands.

Obviously, I didn't want to be disturbed by all that glorious view of the river, so I pulled the thick curtains shut, closed the door to the lounge, turned off the lights, and settled down. This was, looking back, a mistake. Now, if you've never seen Candyman, I won't spoil it, but it involves a very scary Tony Todd terrorising the lovely Virginia Madsen after she stands in front of the mirror and says:

Candyman. Candyman. Candyman. Candyman. Candyman.

Come the end of the film, I was petrified. It was a bit much for my young sensibilities to handle. Something about the film struck a deep and terrible chord in me, and I fled the lounge, pulling the door closed behind me. Because that's where the Candyman lived.

All alone in a dark flat, I tiptoed to the bathroom to go brush my teeth. Except, I couldn't go in. That was where the mirror was, and so Candyman lived in there, too. I couldn't trust myself not to run in there, look in the mirror and blurt out: "Candyman. Candyman. Candyman. Candyman. Candyman."

Brushing my teeth in the corridor, I ducked my head in just long enough to spit and rinse, not daring to make eye contact with the mirror lest I find a hook-handed giant staring back at me. So frightened I could barely breathe, I went to bed, pulled the door closed, and hid under my duvet. What followed were hours of fitful and restless half sleep. I dared not look out from under the covers, because I was almost certain Tony Todd stood at the end of my bed, waiting for me to peek out.

At some point I fell asleep, and that should be the end of the story. Except it's not, because somewhere around three my bedroom door burst open. Petrified, I sat bolt upright, to be confronted by the sight of a towering, hook-handed monster, standing in my doorway, shouting at me to get up.

Except, it wasn't a hook-handed monster. It was my Dad.

I sat up, confused and still terrified. My Dad was not in the habit of waking me up at three in the morning, and he seemed pretty angry about something.

'You've been smoking wacky baccy,' he growled at me.

'What?' I legitimately responded. The party where a joint would be first waved under my nose was still a few years away, and I had absolutely no idea what he was talking about. 'No, I didn't.' I might not have known what he was talking about, but I knew well enough to always offer a firm denial when accused by any adult of a crime or misdemeanour (now known as The Trump Manoeuvre).

My Dad must have seen the absolute confusion on my face, because his anger melted away. He explained that there was a funny smell in the lounge, but that they'd leave things as they were, and see if it still smelled in the morning. I don't think he quite believed me fully, but he left me, heart pounding in my chest, still unsure as to the whereabouts of the Candyman but pretty sure he was under my bed by now.

The next morning, as I rose, bleary-eyed and shredded of nervous system, I held my breath as I left the room. I knew I was in trouble, but still didn't really know why. But I'd made it through the night without the Candyman looming over my bed, and that wasn't nothing.

I brought my breakfast through, noting that the curtains were open once more, bright daylight streaming through them and obliterating any lingering bad feelings I had toward the room. There was no Tony Todd hiding behind the sofa.

'It's okay,' Dad said as I sat. 'We worked out what it was. It was the new pot-pourri. Because the curtains and door were closed, it made the smell build up.'

'Oh,' I said, pleased to be in the clear, but slightly miffed that a bag of dried leaves and twigs were responsible for my 3am terror. Surely if I was going to be terrorised by anything at that hour, it should be something on the scale of the Candyman?

I've never been able to bring myself to re-watch Candyman after all that, but it remains one of the scariest moments in my life, and all because of a bag of dried leaves.

I hope that you're enjoying The Sunset Chronicles so far. This episode has stayed focused on the women of the Chronicles, which is why I'm dedicating this episode to my daughter and my wonderful wife. Two of the strongest, coolest women I know.

JOIN THE HOLLOW STONE

Join my reader's group
and be the first on the planet
to hear about new releases,
and get exclusive content
you won't find anywhere else.

GOT BLOOD?

An apocalyptic storm. A killer on the loose.
The battle for humanity's survival starts here.

About the Author

Paul Stephenson writes pulp fiction for the digital age. His first novel series – the apocalyptic *Blood on the Motorway* trilogy – has been an Amazon bestseller on both sides of the Atlantic. A former journalist, he has a diploma in Creative Writing from Oxford University.

His stories have been featured on the chart-topping horror podcasts, *The Other Stories* and *The Night's End*. His newest project, the ebook serial *The Sunset Chronicles*, is a dystopian sci-fi thriller that will delight and terrify fans of science fiction and horror alike. He is also the creator of the podcast *Bleakwood*, tales of terror from a mysterious English town, and one half of the *All Creatives Now* team, with fellow horror author, Kev Harrison.

He lives in England with his wife, two children, and one hellhound.

To keep up to date with his books, please visit his website PaulStephensonBooks.com

Also by Paul Stephenson

BLOOD ON THE MOTORWAY

Blood on the Motorway

An apocalyptic storm. A killer on the loose. The battle for humanity's survival starts here.

Sleepwalk City

The fight for control has begun. Who will prevail in the battle for humanity's future in the pulse-quickening sequel to Blood on the Motorway?

A Final Storm

The sky is full of lights once more, and the survivors will need more than luck to get them through the coming storm. Who will survive, and who will thrive, in this heart-pounding finale to the Blood on the Motorway saga?

SUNSET CHRONICLES

Plague. Murder. Unrest. Humanity's future looks far from bright.

The year is 2107, and Earth is dying. For Wyn, Lois, and Judd, that's the least of their problems. Each holds a key to Earth's cure and humanity's survival in The Sunset Chronicles, the new sci-fi horror thrill-ride from Paul Stephenson, author of the bestselling British horror saga, Blood on the Motorway.

BLEAKWOOD

Introducing Bleakwood, a horror podcast from the creator of Blood on the Motorway and the Sunset Chronicles.

In the years since the fall, many of us have tried to find out why. To find what lead us here. But with so much of the old world gone, there are more questions than answers. What tore a hole in the world? Can we ever get it back?

But I think I've found something. A binder in the rubble. Don't ask me where. Full of stories about a little town called Bleakwood, stories that seem to show a way that....

They're not in any order, really. And I might be wrong. They might not have the answer. But I think it's in here.

A way back. To the before.

Listen, I'm just going to read them out, and you judge for yourself.

DARE YOU VENTURE INTO BLEAKWOOD?

WHAT TORE A HOLE IN THE WORLD?
CAN WE EVER GET IT BACK?

Find out in Bleakwood, the new horror podcast from the creator of Blood on the Motorway and The Sunset Chronicles

Created and narrated by Paul Stephenson and with stories by some of the most exciting voices in British modern Horror, subscribe to Bleakwood for a fresh story every month.

SCAN ME

www.ingramcontent.com/pod-product-compliance
Lightning Source LLC
Chambersburg PA
CBHW010743210726
48287CB00013B/2995